The Care of Strangers

The
Care of
Strangers

a novel

Ellen
Michaelson

 MELVILLE HOUSE
BROOKLYN · LONDON

The Care of Strangers
Copyright © Ellen Michaelson, 2020
All rights reserved
First Melville House Printing: November 2020

Melville House Publishing   Suite 2000
    46 John Street and   and   16/18 Woodford Rd.
Brooklyn, NY 11201   London E7 0HA

mhpbooks.com
@melvillehouse

ISBN: 978-1-61219-868-2
ISBN: 978-1-61219-869-9 (eBook)

Library of Congress Control Number: 2020943551

Designed by Beste M. Doğan

Printed in the United States of America

1 3 5 7 9 10 8 6 4 2

A catalog record for this book is available from the
Library of Congress

This story is dedicated to the patients of Kings County Hospital whose worldly wiles and audaciousness in the face of illness, poverty, and racism inspired me with their humanity and shaped me as a young doctor and still to this day.

"A novel is not a summary of its plot but a collection of instances, of luminous specific details that take us in the direction of the unsaid and the unseen."

—CHARLES BAXTER, *THE ART OF SUBTEXT*

Part One

Four Fs

Sima pushed a large woman in a wheelchair to the A71 Nurses' Station to catch a bit of breeze. The blackened steel fan was as tall as Sima and stood to the left of a double-wide doorway like an armless guard, stiff and steadfast, the whir and whoosh of its blades a metronome for breathing. Sima lifted her curls to cool the sweat on her neck while she scanned the open ward: beds down one side and up the other, heads to the wall, dark ankles, only a few of them sheet-covered, stuck into the middle of the room, bed after bed, twenty of them. The draft was a relief from the heat but it couldn't clear the smell of roach killer. *Smrod* her mother called it whenever the exterminator made rounds in their building. The reek of *smierdzacy* foot odor and *siki*. Sima preferred the sound of the words for "stink" and "stinky" and "piss" in Polish. She breathed through her mouth.

From behind the Nurses' Station, Nurse Armstrong snapped her fingers. "Stop your daydreaming, young lady."

Sima pulled the chart from the pocket at the back of the wheelchair.

"Bed's ready. On the right, two down from the window."

"Do patients ever ask to be by the window?" "Window" was barely out of Sima's mouth before she realized—what a ridiculous question. Look out the window at what? Beer cans and McDonald's wrappers dug out of trash cans by the bums on Nostrand Avenue in the middle of Brooklyn? "Never mind," she said before Nurse Armstrong had a chance to respond.

She maneuvered her charge through the crowded, *smierdzacy* ward. And then the woman in the wheelchair farted. *Female, fat, fertile, flatulent.* The four Fs of gallbladder disease—Sima could recite them, as she'd heard the medical students do. It had been nearly three years since Chief Resident Danielson invited Sima to join them on rounds after Nurse Armstrong discovered her asleep in the House Staff Library with an anatomy book. Sima had started working double shifts so she could take college courses during the day. She stopped the wheelchair alongside the only empty bed on the ward.

Bella, a nurse's aide, was bent over the bed, folding hospital corners. "Where you been?" A packet of Pall Malls bulged from the pocket of her blue hospital-issue short-sleeved shirt. "I ain't got all night."

"I'm right here," Sima said. She set the squeaky brakes on the wheelchair.

She looked up to see Bella tapping the floor with one foot, staring at her, the same way she'd done on Sima's first day at the County. She hadn't known what to say back then. *You're an expendable nobody, same as me*—that's what she would tell her now, if she had the nerve. Bella knew how to push the weight of her years around. Same as everybody trying to be somebody at the County—the sprawl of twenty-six red brick buildings connected by a tunnel in East Flatbush. That first day Sima walked outside to go for lunch. A-building Medicine, seven stories high, hovered over the entrance of the campus. The windowed bars of the Prison Ward on A32 faced the entrance to the C-building ER, where ambulances drove in. Sima made her way past the defunct hospital sanatorium for tuberculosis, then crossed the driveway to R-building Psych, only two stories with bars on the second-floor windows where they once held the Son of Sam, to the squat cafeteria with its screechy, wooden screen doors. R-building to C-building to A-building: head nurses ordered around floor nurses, and floor nurses unloaded their dirty work on nurses' aides like Bella. And because she didn't have to run all over the hospital between buildings the way orderlies like Sima had to, the high and mighty Bella dumped on Sima whenever she could.

Bullied growing up in Poland on her walk to elementary school by children of anti-Semitic Catholics and communists, Sima didn't care to push anyone around. Even after four years at the County, and never fitting in. The only white girl orderly. She didn't dance to reggae or calypso like the nurses and aides from Jamaica and Trinidad and Tobago. She'd been invited to join them at the end of Saturday night shifts, but the one time she went, she left after an hour. Her Polish-speaking mother would worry. Nights Sima waited for Mama to fall asleep in the living room to crackly recordings of dead Yiddish singers so that she could retreat to her bedroom to study without scrutiny.

Sima watched as Bella finished with the bedsheets. She waited as her patient sat forward in her seat. What an effort it was for the hefty woman to lift herself out of the wheelchair and onto the bed. Even with two hospital gowns tied together, she exposed a belly covered with stretch marks.

Sima stared at the half-moon scar in Miss Osborn's right upper quadrant. "Right upper quadrant"—the medical term for the right side of the abdomen under the rib cage where the liver and gallbladder sit, RUQ. She'd taken Anatomy I and Anatomy II on top of all the pre-med courses Chief Danielson suggested. He made it no secret he would write her a letter of recommendation if she kept her grade point average up. She rarely got less than an A-minus. The scar in the RUQ meant the patient had already had her gall-bladder removed. Something else was wrong.

Once situated on the bed, Miss Osborn lifted her tied-together gowns to air her cornstarch-dusted breasts.

Bella coughed. "You eating all that cornstarch?"

From behind Bella, a tiny voice creaked from the next bed over. "Beer and pork rinds. That's what her kind eats."

Sima smiled. She didn't have to see Alma Mae to recognize the words of the eighty-five-pound asthmatic, Miss Osborn's body opposite, one gown wrapped around her twice and tied in the middle. Repeat patients admitted for days or weeks were treated like royalty. Especially ones who spoke their minds to nurses and aides and sometimes even to the doctors. Alma Mae was in and out of the hospital with asthma every few months. She was tiny but had an opinion about everything and everybody. That cruel comment on Miss Osborn's diet aside, Sima looked forward to hearing what Alma Mae had to say.

Bella elbowed Sima. "Intern wrote orders in the ER to get three stool samples from this one. And you, missy, is going to help me lift old fart face here."

Miss Osborn closed her eyes and sighed the way she had in the elevator.

Alma Mae piped in, "Person stinks of smokes like you ought to know when to keep her mouth shut."

"Sorry," Bella said.

Miss Osborn opened her eyes and looked down at the bedsheets. She didn't say a word.

Sima knew Bella was not sorry, but that piece of knowledge would get her nowhere.

Alma Mae tugged the gray-white ends of her hair into the air. "Leastwise, I got something the doctors know how to treat." Sima pushed her up from the ER every two months it seemed, wheezing and talking and coughing, like she was doing now.

Alma Mae coughed and wheezed again. She couldn't seem to catch her breath.

Bella lifted the oxygen tubing off her pillow. Alma Mae flapped her arms.

"I want Sima," she said. "She's got bedside manner. And she reads anatomy books."

Bella dropped the tubing around the old lady's neck. "We all know how smart Sima is." She smirked and stood back from the bed. "She's all yours, Dr. Sima."

Alma Mae winked. "Sima reads more than books, which is more than I can say for some."

Sima untangled the snake of tubing behind Alma Mae's head. She hid her face behind it so she wouldn't have to respond to Bella's smirk or Alma Mae's wink.

Through the curves of thick plastic, she scanned the ward again. All the beds laid out, a respirator bleeping across the aisle, an IV bag dripping yellow vitamins into Johnson, the alcoholic two beds down, admitted for the second time that summer, the food cart in the middle of the room with half-eaten piles of mashed potatoes and the same brown mystery meat they served in the cafeteria. Nurse Armstrong was making her vital-sign rounds now, demanding patients open their mouths for her thermometer.

Sima placed the oxygen prongs into Alma Mae's nostrils and secured the tubing behind her wrinkled ears. The skin of Alma Mae's neck was as sweaty as Sima's own. A hospital with no air conditioning. Twenty beds to a ward. She'd read it wasn't legal to have huge, open wards anymore, even in inner-city hospitals in the 1980s. Sima often hated this place—the disrespectful patients, the staff talking behind the doctors' backs, the level of illness that was everyday business, the shabby street clothes bagged until discharge. Alma had no teeth. And then every other double shift, Sima loved it.

It was *life*, right-in-your-face life, every ugly and beautiful fragmented bit of it. New York, New York, where people came from every corner of the world. She loved trying to make sense of it. She hated it. She loved it. Deep in the center of Flatbush, the only white member of the ancillary staff. An invisible immigrant. Hardly anyone noticed her slight accent. Her grammar was good enough to pass as American. She *was* an American.

"Sima," Bella said. "Get your skinny white ass over here."

Sima scurried to the foot of Miss Osborn's bed. She patted the sheet over the woman's feet, and as she moved closer, the *smrod* hit. The woman was sitting in a pool of brown, her face covered by her hands.

"It's OK, Miss Osborn," Sima said.

The ward clerk shouted into the room. "Sima, they want you in X-ray."

"Missy, you ain't going nowhere," Bella said.

"Sima's an orderly," Alma Mae piped up. "Call one of them housekeeping folk."

Sima pulled her shoulders back. Alma Mae smiled at her, motioned her toward the door.

She was about to walk away when two interns appeared, stethoscopes flung around their necks. The male, in short sleeves with a royal blue tie, was barking orders at the female, the pockets of her short white intern jacket stuffed with test tubes, rubber gloves, and note cards.

"Sima, they need you *now*," the ward clerk said. "Oh, my Lord, this ward stinks." She stepped toward Miss Osborn's bed and pointed to the brown mess on the floor. And suddenly, the male intern was at the bedside with sterile containers ready to catch his stool samples.

Miss Osborn, now the center of attention, peeked through her fingers at the handsome, eager intern scrambling to remove a red lid on each of his three containers. Bella was on one side of the bed and Sima, still on the other, placed a hand on Miss Osborn's elbow, her skin hot from fever but dry and velvety, the bone a small knob. Sima could only imagine what it was like to lie in a bed with a swarm of nurses and aides and orderlies constantly prodding, doctors young enough to be your own children focused on your oozing stool. She could feel Miss Osborn's arm shake, her whole body.

"It's OK, Miss Osborn," Sima said. "Everything's going to be all right."

Sima didn't know everything was going to be all right. She'd seen how doctors could so easily take hope away. If she'd learned nothing else at the County, she'd come to know that the one thing patients wanted to hold onto was hope. She wasn't sure how much she had for herself in this life, if she'd ever do more than push poor people through the dark hospital hallways on their next desperate trudge. But maybe hope was something.

2

Prosta

Sima set her registration form in front of the clerk at Brooklyn College. The woman raised her right arm, a run of silvery bangles sliding against her white skin, not a hint of tan even though it was still summer. She removed a red pencil from behind her ear. She flicked it between her thumb and forefinger, bangles clanking with each flip of her wrist. PJ Brown, Brooklyn College: her ID didn't identify what she got paid to do.

Sima imagined PJ on the R train, strong-handing a pole by the door so she'd be the first one out at her stop. Big-haired, Brooklyn-born, brassy, New York, New York, from head to toe. Long, shiny fingernails painted twice as red as her day-job pencil. She could see her sauntering out of a bar in spiked heels laughing with loud girlfriends when Sima'd be heading home in sweaty scrubs and sneakers after a night shift. She couldn't picture for herself the kind of American life she conjured for PJ. The woman was no college grad. She boasted to everyone she'd worked the registration desk since the week after she'd given birth. She didn't wear a ring.

But for almost two years now, alongside the official Brooklyn College stamp PJ used on all forms, she kept a photograph: her daughter in cap and gown.

"You see my Sara?" PJ said.

"Of course." Sima needed only one course to graduate. She dreaded seeing the smiling Sara, hugging her diploma.

PJ waved the photograph. "This will be you soon. Make *your* mother proud."

Sima's mother was *prosta*—simple. "Simple people aren't proud," her mother told her in Polish. Sima should be content, a Jew safe in America. How many times had Sima heard this. Her mother with a sixth-grade education only wished her daughter to have "a more better job." Her widowed, single mother didn't want to know her only living child needed to be somebody. She didn't know Sima could soon be a college graduate. Sima was afraid to tell her.

Sima erased English composition from her registration form. But then she didn't put the pencil down. She wrote the course in again. She was not *prosta*. She erased it, she wrote it in.

Tap, tap, tap. PJ rapped on the counter.

"Time's up, dear." PJ took possession. "Deadline was five minutes ago."

Sima watched as PJ placed a firm red check mark in the right upper corner of her form, raised the official Brooklyn College stamp, and pressed it hard over the mark.

"You can change your mind," PJ said. "Drop a course, add another. It doesn't matter." She tossed the form into a box.

Bangles clanked, the window closed.

Sima couldn't remember which courses she'd finally listed, or how many.

The clock overhead said 2:35 p.m.

Only twenty-five minutes until her next shift. She ran down the stairs, out to the Flatbush Avenue subway entrance on Nostrand. Four stops to the County. Four years as an orderly. Four years, four stops. Must be something special about that number. She lived with her mother on the fourth floor in their building. Her mother survived the Holocaust and she wanted four children. She had two miscarriages after the war—four years before Sima was born and four years after. Her mother waited another year, until Sima was five, to have her brother. If her brother had lived, and her father too, they would have been four: Sima, her brother, her father, her mother.

3

Prison Ward

The door to the Prison Ward slammed behind her and she was in a cage without windows. No telephone on the wall, no doorknobs, no way in, no way out. She felt small, an expendable nobody, foreign born, not a gentile. Sima braced herself the moment the second rusty metal door closed her in, before the third one opened and shut, and she was as deep as anyone could be, locked inside the County.

There was a knuckle-shaped dent in the middle of the third door. Above the dent was a small window at the level of her chin. A broad-chested guard with a gun in a holster sat high up behind the window. Black-bean eyes and a tip of pink tongue stuck out between dark lips. His fingers gripped the silvery neck of a microphone.

"Hospital ID," he said.

She lifted her name tag up on her shirt pocket: Orderly Sima. Orderlies didn't rate last names. She wondered what would happen if she lost her ID. Ridiculous thought, she hardly had to prove she was an outsider.

"Closer," the guard said, his words breathy through the microphone.

"I was here last week." She resisted the urge to roll her eyes. She unclipped her badge and held it up against the window.

The guard buzzed her in.

She pushed her stretcher down the hallway, wheels squeaky on the scratched linoleum, past more guards with holsters and billy clubs, posted every ten feet. The ward was at the far end, behind a wall of windows ceiling to floor. A guard stood by the locked door. The Nurses' Station was its own windowed cage, with a separate secure entrance.

"Peabody." Sima heard a woman's voice announce from a microphone. Nurse Bingham. Nurses rated no first name. "Three beds down on the right." She nodded to the guard by the entry to the ward to let Sima in.

"You know the drill," the guard said.

Inside the open ward was filled with dark, moody men doing time at Rikers, street-sick from drugs, from gunshots and stabbings and deeper wounds, the kind nobody could see. She was drawn to these strangers in a way she didn't fully comprehend. She was drawn to County patients wherever they were from, whatever they had lived through.

A husky guard inside the ward stepped beside her, smelling of mustard.

"Stay alert," he said, then stationed himself against the windowed wall, where the move of every prisoner was watched by the guards on the other side.

"We got ourselves another pretty little whitey here!" a grumbly voice shouted. "Why don't these nice lady doctors wear skirts? Show a lonesome man a little leg."

He shot up out of bed and suddenly was up close to Sima. "Hey, hey!" he said.

"Watch it," the guard said, his words out in the air like a cartoon bubble.

The grumbly voice laughed again, and others joined in. Fluorescent lights buzzed from the ceiling.

Sima leaned into her stretcher and moved away, down the aisle between two long rows of beds. The *smrod* was worse than in the women's ward, dirty socks and *siki*. She breathed through her mouth. She stopped where an intern stood over the prisoner she'd come to transport.

She had seen this intern on A71 the day she delivered Miss Osborn. Up close now, Sima thought she could be seeing herself: a young woman with curly, dark hair, narrow shoulders, long arms and fingers. Except for the glasses and the white jacket. The young doctor's pockets bulged: test tubes with red tops, purple tops, and blue ones, 4 x 4 wrapped gauze pads, syringes small and large, rubber gloves. Her chest pocket was over-stuffed with note cards, her pager on the verge of falling off the waistband of her white on-call pants. Mindy Kahn, MD: her ID didn't say she was a psych rotator spending a year on Medicine. Sima had heard the other interns talk. This doctor wasn't anyone she wanted to be mistaken for.

The prisoner sat up against his pillow, his hospital johnny laundered pale, its neckline crooked. He yanked his arm out of the intern's grip.

"Shit, man," the prisoner said. "How many times you going to poke me?"

"It would be nice if you had some veins, Mr. Peabody." Dr. Kahn's demure smile seemed forced. She had one hand on the prisoner's forearm, the other on a tourniquet cinched around his bicep.

"Mr. Peabody," he smirked. He tugged at the tourniquet and it dropped onto the bed sheet. "Mars Peabody's got veins. You just got to know how to find them." He turned to Sima. "What you looking at?"

Sores the size of quarters covered the man's arms. He sat on top of the sheets, hospital bottoms rolled up to his knees. Red wounds ran up one leg and down the other, more than Sima had seen on most addicts at the County. The A71 interns joked that the psych rotator wasn't any good at procedures, she wasn't expected to be, but getting blood out of this addict was going to be a challenge for even the best medical intern.

"What's the matter, doc?" he said to Sima. "Mars Peabody's veins too tough for you?" Then his raspy laugh turned into a cough and a wheeze.

"Give him another pillow," the grumbly voice three beds away spoke up again.

"The doctor needs to listen to his lungs," another prisoner taunted.

"Sit up," Sima said to Mars Peabody. She stepped in close to the bed, reached behind his back with one arm, tilted him forward, and held him upright. "Take a deep breath," she said.

Dr. Kahn stood by Sima's side. "I need to listen to his lungs."

"Doctor! Doctor! Doctor!" A chorus chimed in.

"Pillow! Pillow! Pillow!"

Another guard Sima hadn't noticed was walking down the line of beds. "This ain't no joke," he said. "Peabody can't breathe. Shut up and let the doctor do her job."

Dr. Kahn stood there, arms hanging by her sides the way her stethoscope hung from her neck. She seemed paralyzed by the voices in the room.

Sima kept her hands on Mars Peabody's shoulders. *The laying on of hands*—what she'd read a doctor was supposed to do. What Dr. Kahn needed to do now. Dr. Kahn didn't have one of the extra-long stethoscopes the medical interns used to keep a distance from the patients. She could move in and really hear with this one. Chief Danielson had taught Sima to listen to breath sounds. She wished she had her own stethoscope.

"Sit forward," Sima heard herself say. "Take a deep breath." She could feel his ribs move, the vibration of his wheezing.

Dr. Kahn placed her stethoscope onto the patient's chest. "Deep breath." Mars coughed and wheezed. "Breathe slowly." She listened carefully at several places on his chest. "Smaller breaths," she said, listening from the front and the back. "Slower."

Mars Peabody's breathing eased. Sima couldn't hear his wheezing anymore, she could feel his shoulders relax. And then she felt him squirm forward from her touch.

He closed his hand around the tubing of the stethoscope and stared up at Dr. Kahn.

"My lungs are working just fine now," he said.

They eyed each other, Mars Peabody and Mindy Kahn, MD.

"Time to get that blood you want so badly, don't you think?" he said.

"I don't think so." Dr. Kahn broke the stare and removed his hand from her stethoscope.

"You just got to know how to feel for it," Mars Peabody

said. He grabbed the tourniquet from the bedsheets again. "I can teach you a few things."

He wrapped the tourniquet around his arm, anchoring one end and leaving the other loose. He took the loose end between his teeth and tugged.

"Syringe," he said through the yellow rubber in his mouth. "Come on." He snapped the fingers of his free hand. "You got all them needles on that table. Hook up a big one for me."

"I don't think so," Dr. Kahn repeated.

Sima was impressed with how Dr. Kahn managed to steady her voice. She watched as Dr. Kahn reached for the anchored end of the tourniquet and yanked it, as if she'd been doing this her whole life. The yellow tubing snapped against Mars's skin as it fell off his arm, the other end still held by his teeth.

A strip of skin reddened by the tourniquet stood out from the many sores on his arm.

Mars winced. He fingered the bruised spot. Then he pressed deeper, and deeper again, almost frantically. He shivered and buried his hands under his armpits and rocked.

The tourniquet lay abandoned on the bed sheet.

"Time to get you onto the stretcher, Mr. Peabody," Sima said.

"Mr. Peabody," Mars said. "Mars Peabody." He pulled the bedsheets tightly around him.

4

Hair

A few weeks later, Sima found Dr. Kahn leaning against the counter at the A71 Nurses' Station, writing in a chart. Since the Prison Ward, Dr. Kahn had clearly learned to fill her pockets more carefully: three-by-five patient note cards were now neatly clipped together in her chest pocket with a penlight, a small notebook stood unruffled in one side pocket, new packaged 4 x 4 gauze pads reached over the top of the other. A clean tourniquet looped through a buttonhole in her short white jacket, fresh from the laundry.

Dr. Kahn's hair was much darker than Sima's, curlier and frizzy. So unlike the billboard blondes hovering over the heads of America she saw everywhere when she first arrived as a child. On their first Sunday in Brooklyn, in their basement apartment, her Aunt Miriam flipped open a shiny magazine to page after page of slinky women with silky blond hair, placed an even shinier box in her mother's lap, and told her mother that the shampoo in the box would make her a real American. Her mother's baby sister, Miriam, who married the first man in their village who agreed to take her to the United States, untied the scarf on her head, her hair now a soft blond, and twirled around the room.

In Poland, everybody was blond, *shikse* blond, her mother said, and she would have none of it. She shoved the shiny box onto the floor, told Miriam to cover her shame, and warned her to keep her hands off Sima. In junior high school, with the help of a girl she barely knew, Sima tried to iron her tresses. She wouldn't be a blonde but she could have long, straight hair like Cher. Sima was relieved that now, in the '80s, women, in New York had perms—they all wanted curly hair. But not frizzy and disheveled the way Dr. Kahn's was.

"New York summers are good for curly hair," Sima said.

Dr. Kahn contorted her neck, attempting to tame unruly strands behind one shoulder.

"I stopped using a hair dryer," Sima said. "You should just let it go."

Dr. Kahn flipped a page in the chart and kept writing.

"I'm told my curly hair is softer than an Amsterdam hippy." *Amsterdam hippy.* She had no clue where this idea came from. She paced behind Dr. Kahn. "Jewish hair is not as frizzy as Italian. You're Jewish, right?"

Dr. Kahn didn't raise her eyes. "They asked me that in Massachusetts." She closed one chart, set it aside, and opened another one. "Nobody asks me in New York."

"I'm writing a paper on ethnic hair."

Dr. Kahn turned to face Sima. "Once when I was in high school, waiting at bus stop, a man asked me if I was Italian or Greek or Moroccan or Brazilian. When he ran out of countries, he asked me if I was Jewish. He said 'Jewish' almost in a whisper, as if he'd uncovered my big secret."

Dr. Kahn tapped her pen on the chart. "So what are you writing this paper for?"

"English composition." Sima had put off taking the course, afraid she'd fail. But it was now or never. It was the last course she needed to graduate—she hadn't told anyone. She hadn't told anyone she wanted to drop out. "I've had an interest in hair since I was six, when I first moved here from Poland."

"My grandfather was born in Poland," Dr. Kahn said. "Every time I see him, he says, 'So when are you going to get a haircut?'"

"Isn't that what mothers say to sons these days?"

"Not in my family. Only daughters, and I'm the first-born. My parents were going to name me David."

"My parents wanted me to be David, too," Sima said. After her brother David died, her father sometimes called her David, Dave, Davey. "Your hair is frizzy for Jewish hair."

Dr. Kahn's pen rolled off the counter onto the floor. "Well, damn," she said. "Who cares?"

"In Poland they cared." Sima looked straight at Dr. Kahn. "They didn't ask me politely what country I was from. They called me a kike. A Christ killer. I was only six."

Dr. Kahn bent to the floor to retrieve her pen. When she stood, her cheeks were flushed, as much as Sima's. She focused on her chart and started to write again. Without making eye contact she said softly, "In New York everybody's hair is dark and curly, but in Boston it's brown or blond, and straight."

Sima stared at the toe of her running shoe where it hit the wall of the Nurses' Station and left a mark. "I've never been to Boston," she said.

"You've got to get out of New York," Dr. Kahn said.

Sima had barely been across the Brooklyn Bridge to Manhattan. She'd never stepped foot on Staten Island or in the Bronx. She went to Queens by mistake once when she got on the wrong subway line. She had to take a bus and it took her an extra hour to get home. She'd hardly ever taken a bus since she was a child, since her first years in America.

5

Tea for Two

When Sima was seven, she and her mother boarded the B82 bus to Canarsie. It was 1967 and they'd been in New York a year when Mrs. Puretz, the other Polish-speaking Jewish widow in their building, told her mother about Canarsie, where her daughter lived in a stand-alone house with her *przystojny maz* and two *piekny dziatki*. Good-looking husband and beautiful children. And a long-haired Dachshund, just like the one Mrs. Puretz had given her daughter on her tenth birthday in Poland that was viciously run over by the Ukrainian man next door. Canarsie was *wporsazdku*. Safe. Three times a week the widow Puretz walked five blocks to catch the bus on Avenue K. It was a fifteen-minute ride. *Cudowny.* Marvelous. Sima's mother had managed to negotiate a good price for her dead husband's collection of blue glass and silver to purchase two one-way tickets to America on a huge boat across the Atlantic on her own with her little daughter tightly in tow. But a year later, Sima had to be by her side if her mother ventured out of their Kings Highway neighborhood. Her mother demanded Sima check the signs at the bus stop three times to be sure they boarded in the correct direction.

They got off the B82 near Avenue L and walked the bustling street. Her mother clutched her purse to her chest in one hand, Sima's arm in the other. She refused to go inside any of the stores. And then she stopped in front of a thrift shop. Her legs were tired, she said. She stood staring in the window. She pointed to a pair of glass tea cups with silver holders. Just like ones she'd sold for passage to America, a set of six that she and her friends drank tea from every afternoon in their village in Poland.

"Jak duzo? Jak duzo?" She tapped on the window until Sima read the price tag.

Her mother opened her purse. Without her usual hesitation, she counted out the necessary cash into her seven-year-old daughter's hand. She waited outside while Sima made the purchase. When they returned home from Canarsie, her mother headed to the kitchen. Still in her coat, she washed the vintage Russian glass cups, dried them with the lime-green linen towel reserved for the few special items she'd secreted from Poland. The handles and the holders on the thrift shop acquisitions were only silver plated, her mother pointed out, not the real *Podstakanniki,* and so they wouldn't get as hot.

Her mother set the two sparkling pieces of glass on the table. She scooped a large spoonful of tea leaves into one cup and drowned the leaves with boiling water. Sima stared at the steam swirling above the surface of the cup, waiting and waiting for the tea to steep. Finally her mother dipped a finger in. She declared it was cool enough to drink, and presented Sima with a few sips from the large spoon. Sima would have to wait until she was older to drink from the glass cup herself. When she was eight, her mother said she wasn't quite old enough. At ten, her mother told she had to wait until she was twelve. On her twelfth birthday, her mother told her thirteen was the proper age to start drinking tea.

From the time Sima was tall enough to stand over the stove, she hovered over the unpainted kettle every afternoon, steam from the spout threatening to frizz her hair, until the whistle blew. Their daily ritual. But by thirteen, Sima had lost interest in tea, in her mother's silver-handled glassware. She never poured for herself, she never sat.

"Turn off the *pisk!*"

"Yes, Mama."

Sima liked the Polish word for "shriek" even though her mother shouted it from the kitchen table a foot away.

"*Usiac*, Sima." Sit.

Sima set the steaming glass cup alongside the lace napkin in front of her mother.

"Not today, Mama." Sima spoke in English at tea-time. Sima dressed in scrubs at teatime now, about to leave for her next double shift. What she loved was to get to the hospital early when she worked days, to stand in line with the doctors and nurses at the Greek diner truck outside the ER. For a dollar she could buy a warm raisin bagel in a brown paper bag and coffee in a paper cup with the blue Greek diner design. Once in a while, she'd splurge on a cheese Danish, an American pastry her mother refused to eat.

6

Fever Workup

Double shifts and on-call shifts, like Jewish holidays, start at night. But the beginning of a Jewish holiday is calm: table set for a family dinner, white candles in silver holders passed down one generation to the next, ready to be lit. The start of a night at the County was more like Sima's childhood in Poland: chaotic—pagers beeping, swallows of dinner abandoned, feet scurrying in their call to action.

Sima made her way through the cafeteria line, her plate piled with eggplant parmesan, one of the few County meals she liked, free with hospital ID. She stopped by Dr. Kahn, alone at a table. She had seen Dr. Kahn's name posted on the A71 on-call schedule and asked to work the same night. She was pleased when the curly-haired psych intern nodded for Sima to join her. But almost immediately, Dr. Kahn's pager went off. She closed the Styrofoam carryout container she'd filled with eggplant in anticipation of this moment, shoved it into a plastic bag with fork and napkin, and without a word, headed for the door. Sima sat by herself for not more than five minutes before she too was paged to the ER.

Screams blared in the hallway outside the Female Room. They came through the open door from a bony sixteen-year-old girl squirming on a gurney. The smooth-skinned teenager was sweaty and tender to the touch everywhere the nurses laid a finger. It was the sickle cell anemia *pisk* of painful bones. A human shriek. The sound of squashed red blood cells, oxygen-deprived, stuck in tiny capillaries throughout the body. The girl's eyes bulged. Her arms wrapped around the side rails of the bed, skinny but strong as a wrestler's, yanking so hard the gurney shook. Sima figured the nurses hadn't given her Demerol yet. Or not enough.

The girl was Dr. Kahn's first admission for the night, and Sima's first transport. Together they waited until the girl got a shot of Demerol and the nurses made it clear it was time to move her out. Dr. Kahn studied the chart. Sima pushed the gurney to the elevator. The girl's *pisk* did not let up.

Mr. Biggs, the night shift elevator man, held his door open until the gurney was in, Sima and Dr. Kahn squeezed alongside it. He tapped his foot to the sound of the girl's screams the way he did when he wasn't busy, listening to jazz from the boom box he kept under his chair. The girl raised her refrain an octave higher. Mr. Biggs kept tapping until the girl began to wave her arms and socked him with her IV pole.

"Hey, young lady," he said to the girl. He moved the IV arm back onto the gurney. The girl pulled against his grip. She opened her mouth wide like a baby crow, and out came an even louder cry. "Nurses forgot to restrain this one."

"Sima can hold her arm," Dr. Kahn said.

Newbie intern, Mr. Biggs mouthed silently. Sima nodded.

"You the doctor." He shook his bald head. "You be the one have to put in a new IV when she yanks this one out." He rearranged the gold earring in his left ear and straightened the shiny chain around his neck. He reached for his boom box. "Maybe some tunes will help."

Sima placed a hold on the girl's forearm. Her wrist was so skinny she could reach around it entirely. The ER should have sent her to Pediatrics but there were no beds. Busy, busy night, and it was barely dinnertime.

Dr. Kahn stepped off the elevator first. Sima backed the gurney out and pushed it down the long hallway behind her. The girl had quieted. But as soon as they stopped at the Nurses' Station, she began screaming again.

The night nurse lifted her clipboard. "Five IVs out," her musky voice boomed over the girl's. "Bed nine, bed six, bed five. And eight and twelve from before."

Bad luck for the intern on call. There wasn't enough

staff to keep an eye on every patient's arm. Replacing the IVs alone threatened to take up half of Dr. Kahn's night since there was no IV team at the County, just as there was no blood drawing team. Sima had heard the medical interns snicker at Dr. Kahn's talent for inserting lines, far below a passable flair for tough sticks. She wished she had this skill so she could help Dr. Kahn.

"And bed eleven, your favorite, Miss Osborn. IV is ok but her temp's 103. Still."

"Miss Osborn's back?" Sima said.

"Yes, ma'am." The night nurse squinted over her spectacles.

"Put the screamer next to the respirator."

Dr. Kahn had so many things to do. Sima could feel her hold on the side rails of the gurney as if a tight grasp would make the night move faster as they pushed to the empty bed alongside the noisy respirator with its bellows bellowing, past Alma Mae, who was also back again, and Miss Osborn. Together they lifted the girl off the gurney onto the bed. Her hospital gown slipped off her shoulders, over her clavicles, down her chest, exposing barely budding breasts. Sima resettled the gown over the girl's torso and retied it around her neck. The girl began to squirm in the bed. She waved her IV arm in the air.

"You don't want to lose her IV, too," Sima said.

Dr. Kahn plugged into her stethoscope.

"I want my mamma!" The *pisk* of a six-year-old.

Sima got hold of the IV arm. The girl lay still a moment. Then she flailed the other arm.

"She needs Demerol." Sima pointed to the foot of the bed. "The nurse left a restraint."

Dr. Kahn cinched the ragged piece of white sheet around the girl's wrist. She screamed louder. Dr. Kahn leaned in with her stethoscope, a futile exercise. She stopped making noise long enough to lunge forward and close her teeth on the psych intern's thumb.

"Damn it," Dr. Kahn said. The girl wouldn't let go.

Sima placed both hands firmly on the girl's chin and pried her jaw open.

The night nurse appeared at the foot of the bed, a chart in one hand and a syringe in the other. "I need an order for that restraint." She glanced at Dr. Kahn grasping her thumb. "And for the Demerol fifty, with twenty-five of Vistaril."

The nurse lifted the hospital gown, cooed to the girl, and jabbed her in the buttocks. The girl's eyes were wide, wet with tears. With her hands tied, she couldn't wipe them. She rolled to her side and settled in, a veteran. Her legs were splayed as though she were running in place. One of her tied arms trailed behind her.

Sima pulled the gown over the girl's exposed skin. She unfolded the light summer blanket at the foot of the bed and spread it over the sick child.

"You'll need a shot of Keflex for that thumb," the night nurse said. She unwrapped a gauze pad and handed it to Dr. Kahn. "Not every night a nurse gets to jab an intern." She chuckled and placed the open chart on the corner of the bed. "Don't forget to sign the order for the restraint and the Demerol, doctor. And for the antibiotic. I'll have it for you up front."

Sima stood at the head of the bed. Dr. Kahn leaned against the wall to one side, cradling her injured thumb. They watched the girl breathe, eyes closed, her skinny limbs askew under the blanket, one dark foot uncovered.

"Have you noticed how little hair black people have on their bodies?" Sima said.

"Koreans have even less." Dr. Kahn snugged the gauze on her thumb. "I'm doing my own study. Men and hair: where they have it and where they don't."

"Yeah?" Sima grinned.

"Now that I'm in New York, I get to go out with lots of different ethnic types."

"You have time to date?"

"Not really," Dr. Kahn said. "But I met a Korean guy this summer. He had the thickest hair on his head but hardly any on his legs. Or anywhere else for that matter."

Classmates at Brooklyn College joked about how hairy Jewish men were. Sima didn't date. Her father had hairy knuckles but she couldn't recall much more about his looks than what she'd seen in the black-and-white photographs her mother kept hidden in a drawer in the dining room.

"Jewish men are hairy," Sima said.

"I dated a tennis pro in college," Dr. Kahn said. "He was surprisingly hairy. Fourth-generation American. Someone in his family fought in the Civil War."

"I've never met anyone more than second-generation American."

"Like I said, you've got to get out of New York."

ON HER WAY OFF THE ward, Sima stopped at Alma Mae's bed to reposition her oxygen tubing. One bed over, Dr. Kahn sat in a chair, stretching an extra-long tourniquet, supplies set up for three sets of blood cultures.

"Please make a fist, Miss Osborn," Dr. Kahn said.

"Sima, you better help that new doctor," Alma Mae said.

Miss Osborn smiled at Sima. "I seen you before. You good."

"Interns draw blood, not orderlies," Dr. Kahn stated. A dubious County honor.

Alma Mae ignored Dr. Kahn's remark. "Honey," she said to Miss Osborn, "she's as good as any of them doctors. She's going to be one herself soon enough."

Sima was startled. "I'm only an orderly," she said. "I have to graduate college first."

"You make rounds with them doctors," Alma Mae said. "I seen you."

"The Chief Resident is just being nice." Sima didn't want Dr. Kahn to hear.

"You only got to finish that English class," Alma Mae said. "That's what you told me." Alma Mae had a way of making it easy for Sima to confide, and never forgot a word. This tiny woman knew more about her than her own mother.

Dr. Kahn seemed preoccupied. She tied the tourniquet snugly. "Please keep making a fist, Miss Osborn." She slapped at the bulging skin to plump the big vein there. She released the tourniquet, moved it, and retied it. Miss Osborn pulled her arm away.

"My fingers turning blue." Miss Osborn slapped Dr. Kahn's hand as she loosened the tourniquet another time. "I want Sima."

Dr. Kahn shoved the tourniquet into a pocket, collected her supplies and stepped away.

"Hey," Miss Osborn sat taller against her pillow. "You going to take care of me?"

Dr. Kahn turned back to her. "You have a fever. We're trying to find out why."

"They took my shit to the lab," she said. "Didn't that tell what's wrong?"

"I wish it did. For both our sakes," Dr. Kahn said. "We

need to get blood. Sometimes it's hard to see veins under black skin."

"I don't see nobody here who's not black. You sure you a doctor?"

Dr. Kahn's face went blank. She hadn't done any psych rotations yet, but Sima expected her to think more carefully before she spoke. She'd handled herself better on the Prison Ward.

"Squeeze my hand," Sima said, "while Dr. Kahn puts the tourniquet on again."

Miss Osborn sighed. She let her arm go loose and gripped Sima's hand.

Dr. Kahn set her supplies back on the bed and sat down slowly. She didn't look up as she retrieved the tourniquet from her pocket and cinched it tight. She pressed her fingers on the patient's skin. Her eyes, her white coat, her nose, every part of her doctor-self appeared aimed at the target. "It's sometimes hard to find a vein in a large arm."

"I'm sure there's one in there," Miss Osborn said.

Sima marveled at the way County patients mustered their reserves. Doctors too.

Dr. Kahn removed the tourniquet. She walked around the bed and tied off Miss Osborn's other arm and palpated for a vein there. She freed that arm, and walked off the ward. She returned a few minutes later with additional supplies: more 4 x 4s, more gloves, half a dozen large twenty-cc syringes, and the longest needles she could fine.

"Maybe you should page the senior," Sima said.

"This is intern's work," Dr. Kahn said.

"You're a psych rotator," Sima said. "No one cares if you can't do everything." Sima knew Dr. Kahn was aware of how much her survival on the medical wards depended on being competent at these menial tasks that made a County intern's life hell, especially the nights. But sometimes being competent meant asking for help. "It's ok to ask for help."

The night nurse stationed herself at the foot of bed with an update. "Fever Bed 1, temp 101. IV's out, too."

Dr. Kahn didn't respond. She took off her white jacket and hung it over the back of the chair. "Please lie back," she said to Miss Osborn. The nurse headed off to other tasks.

Dr. Kahn stepped to the head of the bed. She cranked it down until Miss Osborn was lying flat. She opened a clean pair of sterile gloves and stretched them on. She moved one hand deep into the folds of flesh between the patient's pendulous abdomen and her wide thigh.

"Nerve, artery, vein," Dr. Kahn mumbled under her breath the mnemonic Sima heard medical students recite. Dr. Kahn was feeling for the artery that pulsed alongside the vein.

During emergencies, doctors drew blood from the groin to check a blood sugar or hemoglobin. But interns were taught to avoid getting samples for blood cultures from dirty sites, places on the body where it was impossible to sterilize the skin. The groin was one of those sites. Bacteria in the area often contaminated the cultures, making the results useless.

"You should page the senior resident," Sima said. Drawing blood from a dirty site for a fever work was worse than not even trying to do the dreaded task on the on-call intern's endless list of scut work. The night was growing longer. And Sima had her own work to do.

7

Identity Displacement Syndrome

The first Monday of every month, Sima worked days, and her shift started in Psychiatry. The stairwell in R-building was grimy linoleum and bits of fossilized gum, the *smrod* of urine instead of stool. Sima breathed through her mouth one flight up to the Psych ER. Behind a curtained-off space, a patient who called himself JJ lay stretched out on a gurney, his bony knees poking up out of baggy shorts. His ankles descended into American Flyer high-tops.

"I'm training to be a Jew," JJ said. "Are you a Jew?"

Fever beads, sweat rosary of the sick, covered his forehead. His admission papers read: "Fever, rash, Identity Displacement. r/o meningitis (Puerto Rican street kid wants to be a Jew)."

"Like my yarmulke?" JJ tapped the red-and-black beanie pinned to his mop of kinky, dyed, red-brown hair. Sima had hid her own hair under a cap for two months after trying to become a blonde without Aunt Miriam's help. The tint turned her locks green in the pool at the Y. She finally convinced her mother, after two weeks that wearing the cap to bed was part of a school assignment.

"I got a Jewish nose, don't you think?" JJ said. He turned his head sideways. "Just like Sammy."

"Sammy?" Sima said.

"Sammy Davis, Jr.," JJ said.

"So you want to be a singer?" Sima said.

"I want to be rich and famous," JJ said.

"Most Jews aren't rich and famous." None Sima knew. "And they don't like their noses."

She felt JJ's shiver through the edge of the bed. She tapped the shoulder of an aide.

"Can we get this patient a blanket?"

The aide's baby-blue shirt was opened halfway down his hairy chest. "Go ask a nurse," he said and rolled an empty wheelchair alongside the gurney. "We need the bed. Put him in this."

"He's got a fever," Sima said. JJ's arm was as warm and sweaty as Miss Osborn's. "He needs a blanket."

The aide grabbed a sheet from a pile on the counter and dumped it on the wheelchair.

JJ lay on the gurney, blue-lipped. "Nobody can tell I

wasn't born a Jew. I got the proof. I got the nose." He curled up like a baby and closed his eyes.

Sima smoothed the sheet to his neck and got a close-up of *the nose*. There was a small bump in it but it didn't compare. Sammy's was squashed in from being smacked, Sima was sure of it. No big ugly hook at the end like the cartoons of Jewish noses in the Polish newspaper her father had insisted she clip every week for his file.

The aide bumped the wheelchair into the gurney.

JJ opened his eyes. "Nobody bumps Sammy Davis, Jr." His arms were folded under the sheet, his eyes fixed on the line of fluorescent ceiling lights.

"This ain't no Vegas, Sammy," the aide aid. "Give up the bed."

SIMA STEERED JJ INTO THE tunnel hallway, *klaps-klaps*, the slap-slap of her running shoes on the concrete floor, creating an echoing beat, the scrape of the wheelchair wheels making bad music. JJ, alternately shivering and sweating, hummed to the beat of the wheels.

Heading toward them was the short, skinny guy with spiky hair and headphones plugged into a Walkman hanging from the waistband of green scrubs. He strutted to his music, cracking gum, and stared at Sima. Tunnel Guy:

he moved so quickly she never saw a name tag, only the word MAINTENANCE in small black letters across the back of his shirt as he passed by. They never spoke. She only saw him in the tunnel. He reminded her of some leftover hazy childhood fear of wandering in dark, scary places on her own. There was something about the way he strutted, ghostlike, past the old cages that lined the tunnel under the Psych building. Rumors told they used to put the uncontrollable crazies in these cages before there were drugs to keep them quiet. She saw Tunnel Guy so infrequently that his presence haunted her, the way she imagined her father had been haunted by government officials after the Holocaust. Crazy JJ didn't pay him any notice.

JJ yawned like a cat. "My real name is Jose Iglesias Juarez," he said. "But you can call me Sammy."

"Yeah," Sima said. "And you can call me Dave."

Dave, *Davey*—she could hear her father's voice. His only son named after his only brother who died before his fifteenth birthday. And then her father lost the second Davey at less than two weeks old.

Pipes lined the tunnel hallway, wrapped in white like mummies. Steam seeped from the seams the way it did from manholes on the streets. God of the ghetto gone underground, connecting the twenty-six buildings of the County under the sidewalks and the trees, coming out in hot puffs from pipes carrying water from A-building to C-building to R-building.

JJ reached over the armrest of the wheelchair and grabbed for one of the pipes.

"Don't touch," Sima said. "They're hot. See the yellow DANGER sign?"

"I like all this steam." JJ sniffed the musty tunnel air and raised his arms overhead, palms up, as if pleading with his maker. "Looks like heaven."

"Jews don't exactly believe in heaven," Sima said.

"So what makes a person a Jew?" JJ asked.

God of the Puerto Ricans gone underground. God of the Jamaicans and God of the Haitians and God of the good people of Trinidad and Tobago. And then she heard herself say, "Jews are circumcised when they're eight days old."

SIMA WAS FIVE WHEN DAVEY was born and they all climbed down the narrow steps to the under-the-ground where there were no windows, only the light of candles. Her mama and papa, and the seven Jewish men in their village remaining after the war, with their wives and children. There was no rabbi, there was no moyel, the man who circumcised Jewish baby boys. So her papa's friend, Lesk, the bookbinder, opened his yellow-brown pages to the Hebrew words he read every time one of the wives gave birth to a *chlopak* and everyone came to the under-the-ground to announce the child's name and watch Lesk make the cut in the pink, wrinkly skin to bring another Jewish boy's soul into the world.

"It's dangerous," Mama said, "if the Poles see his little body. I don't know why we bother. It makes no difference. He's my son, so that makes him Jewish. Jewish enough."

"In the eyes of God it makes a difference," Papa said.

"He won't be Jewish in any other way," Mama said.

"*Sha!*" Papa said. Be quiet. "Hold down your son and stand proud." Her papa nudged her mama to help Lesk's wife hold down her brother's little pink legs.

"I won't," Mama said. "I can't." She sat down and started to cry.

Lesk's wife nodded and Papa sat, but when he put his arms around his wife, she pushed him away. Lesk's wife reached for Sima's hand and pulled her to the table where her brother lay. Legs and penis in the air, tiny tongue out between toothless gums, dark hair in curlicues covering his head.

"You hold the right leg, Sima," Lesk's wife said. "I'll hold the left one."

Lesk's silver knife hung in the air like a sword. And Lesk was a strong, brave knight. He closed his eyes and said the blessing. "*Da-veed,*" he announced her brother's Hebrew name. His face shiny with sweat, he held the knife in one hand, and pulled on the wrinkly foreskin with his other. A drop of sweat landed on the baby's belly. And then a sliver of skin fell off the newborn penis, and then tiny drops of blood.

Sima's brother let out a *pisk* worse than she had ever heard. His legs kicked, his body squirmed, he wailed. She tried so hard to hold the leg that she started to cry and lost her grip.

"It's OK, little one, it's OK," Lesk's wife said. She stroked the baby's head and let go of the other leg. She dipped her pinkie into the silver goblet on the matching tray where her husband had put down his knife, alongside the sliver of foreskin. She touched the wine on her fingertips to the baby's wide-open, wailing lips. "It's ok."

She dabbed drops of blood off the smooth, exposed skin and covered the now-Jewish penis with a piece of white gauze. She bundled Sima's brother in a blanket and rested him in his mama's arms.

Her mama was crying and her brother was crying and Sima was crying, along with everyone in the under-the-ground. They were drinking wine and crying.

JJ CUPPED HIS HANDS OVER his crotch and spoke in a serious tone. "What about girl Jews?"

"If your mother is a Jew, then you're a Jew," Sima said.

"Are you a Jew?" JJ said. He pointed at Sima. "You got the nose."

God of the Puerto Ricans talking to the God of the Jews. Hair. Penis. Nose. Sima could feel her face getting hot. She was safe as a Jew in America, with her nose, her hair. But life was more than safety. They needed to keep moving. She drove the wheelchair forward through the steam and the pipes, around the corner, past the cages.

JJ lifted the sheet and reached a hand into his baggy shorts. "I'm a Jew," he said.

"I don't need to know that." She kept her eyes on the hallway ahead, pushed harder.

"Why not?" JJ said.

And then they were stopped in front of the elevators. There was no place to go. He was crazy, she told herself. Harmless. She wanted to tie the sheet to the armrests of the wheelchair but she was afraid to touch him.

"Maybe we're cousins," JJ said. "Wouldn't you want to know that? There's a synagogue in San Juan," he said. "I seen it. Jews from everywhere."

She and her mother could have moved to San Juan instead of New York. And her mother would still only be speaking Polish.

JJ was shivering again. She fingered the sheet, tugged it free from where it was stuffed on one side of the wheelchair seat and draped it around his shoulders and over his private parts.

Elevator Lady Miss Lawrence stood by her open door. "What have we got here?"

JJ sat back. He drew his wayward hand into a polite position and gathered the sheet in close to his chest. "One Jew helping another," he said.

"Never seen a Jew with red hair," Miss Lawrence said. "What do you say, Sima?"

JJ nodded at Sima. "I knew it."

Sima backed the wheelchair into the elevator, away from Miss Lawrence's gaze. She leaned against the rear wall thinking it was easier for a Jew to look American than it was for a Puerto Rican to look like a Jew. Maybe she should become a singer, memorize the Yiddish songs her mother loved so much, go to Juilliard instead of medical school. She had no talent for music.

8

This and That

Whether the elevator was working or not, Sima took the stairs to the apartment she shared with her mother, the same four flights to the same apartment they'd lived in since 1966. She stopped the way she always did on each floor to see what magazines neighbors had left in the trash by the stoop doors. The walk and the stops gave her time to think about her day, to make her transition from school or the hospital to that fourth-floor apartment she otherwise rarely left. It had been several days since she'd transported JJ. His Puerto Rican yarmulke, his dyed red hair, his nose—she couldn't get him out of her mind. She took her time more than usual that evening. But she was never in a rush to see her mother after a long day at the County or as many hours as she could fit in at the Brooklyn College library. To sit with her mother at the kitchen table not speaking, the television her mother didn't understand always on in the background, or the crackly recordings of dead Yiddish singers. Not speaking about so many things.

In the neighbor's trash next door, on top of a pile of *New York Times*, she saw last week's *New York Magazine*. Several years before, she'd brought home a discarded copy of the "flashy" publication. Her mother had chased her around the apartment. *"Szmira!"* she screamed. Her mother would have cheered if she'd come home with an issue of the *Forward*, world famous voice of immigrants of the Jewish ghetto. Even if it weren't the Yiddish edition, the only one her mother could barely read. Her mother grabbed the magazine and Sima stormed out of the apartment. Her mother followed her down the hallway into the elevator of their Kings Highway building, waving the slick pages in the air, yelling at the top of her lungs. "You're a good girl, a Jewish girl! No steal this *szmira!*"

When the elevator door opened one floor down, her short, stout mother smiled at Mrs. Puretz, equally short and stout, who stepped in. Her mother stood at the back wall like the survivor she was and switched to a quiet Polish.

"For this, we didn't come to America. Your father didn't die for *this.*"

Mrs. Puretz, the only other Polish-speaking widow left in the building, clutched her purse to her ragged woolen coat. Her weekly trips to Canarsie stopped when her grandchildren were grown; her daughter didn't have much time for her now. She nodded at Sima's mother.

"No die for this." Her proud, broken English. She turned to Sima. "Your mama knows."

She'd done it once again. Sima's very private mother never passed up an opportunity to engage a Polish-speaking Jewish stranger in their arguments about how to behave in America.

Sima would never forget her roots. But her mother didn't believe her. And she didn't understand how much Sima needed to fit in somewhere, *anywhere*, in New York, New York, center of the universe according to numerous cartoons pinned to the bulletin board in the Brooklyn College library. New Yorkers so proud to be New Yorkers. At least the natives were. She had no point of reference. As she told Dr. Kahn, she had never stepped foot outside of Brooklyn except to Manhattan since she'd arrived off the boat at the age of six. She had never even been to Staten Island.

This—this reading of a particular American magazine— was the most ambitious way Sima had ever openly defied her mother, defied anyone. She was a lonely outsider—at the County, at college, wherever she went. Maybe she needed to move out. She could ask Dr. Kahn if she needed a roommate. She was not simple, like her mother. She was smart. But she had no idea how she could tell her lonely, *prosta* mother she was about to graduate college.

SHE PICKED UP THE DISCARDED *New York Magazine* and hid it under her coat. She pulled the key of out of her pocket and turned the lock in the apartment door. There were no lights on; her mother was still out shopping. She hung her key on a hook by the door. She was about to stuff the magazine into her backpack, but then she placed it on the center of the dining room table.

She dropped the backpack on the floor, didn't bother to take off her coat and hat. She went directly to the dining room cabinet where her mother kept the few family heirlooms they had left: a set of silver spoons that had belonged to her mother's mother; a candelabra, also silver, etched with a delicate floral pattern; six small silver cups for Passover and one larger one for Elijah; five ivory napkins; her father's yarmulke, one side hand-knitted by her mother with blue velour backing; one blue glass salt and pepper shaker. Blue was her father's color. These precious heirloom pieces Sima had studied so many times when her mother was out. She had touched, held, counted every item; she had memorized where each sat in the large drawer in the middle of the cabinet. She knew the story behind each and every single one.

Sima reached for the handle of the narrow drawer on the left side of the cabinet, the secret drawer she'd been forbidden as a child to touch. And still not invited to share. Where her mother kept the photographs Sima was not allowed to see. Since that first time her mother caught her in the drawer, after the *New York Magazine* fiasco, she had respected her mother's wishes. Now she held the handle and pulled back on it very slowly so as not to disturb the contents. She didn't want to tear anything, especially not a photograph.

She stood over the open drawer. An ivory napkin was there—it must have been the sixth missing from the set of five in the larger middle drawer. She lifted the napkin and found an envelope. The edges were curled up, yellowed. There were several smaller envelopes, one on top of the other, not placed in any neat, orderly fashion but lounging as if tossed there and forgotten.

She opened the largest envelope on top. It contained papers with "US Government" written in fancy type. They were immigrant documents. Papers giving Sima and her mother permission to become US citizens. A letter with a seal on it stating that Aunt Miriam was their sponsor. Another letter stating that her mother had been allowed to become a citizen even though she couldn't speak or read English, and that her daughter, Sima, then nine years old, was thereby granted citizenship too.

Even more carefully, Sima lifted the next envelope from the drawer. In it was a black and white photograph of her parents, standing like statues in front of their house in Poland, Sima situated in the middle, holding hands with both of them. Sima didn't know if she remembered what the house looked like or just had memories of it from what little her mother had told her. There was another photograph of her father as a teenager and a boy who looked like his clone, half a head shorter. That must have been Uncle David, who died before Sima was born. In a third envelope were photographs of people smiling with raised glasses in their hands.

She was about to open a small envelope when she heard a key in the door and the squeak of the knob. She stood like a statue over the drawer, her breath suddenly faster, the beat of her heart in her ears. Then, without daring to look up, she gathered the photos and the envelopes and set them back in the large drawer as quickly and carefully as she could. And turned around to see her mother heading across the room, her eyes aimed at the center of the dining room table.

Sima reached for the glossy magazine, her fingers sticking to the sleek cover as she leaned over her backpack where it rested against a leg of the table, and stuffed it away, the way she stuffed all her thoughts and dreams and fears and sorrow.

"What you put in your pack?" her mother said in Polish, in her usual prickly tone.

"This and *that*, Mama," she said. "Just this and *that*. It's time for tea. You want tea?"

"Tea," her mother said. "Tea before dinner. Always."

That morning before her shift, she had splurged on a cheese Danish. She had time to finish her cup of coffee, but half the Danish wrapped in a torn piece of saran wrap was in a brown paper bag at the bottom of her backpack. She hoped it wouldn't be stale by the next morning.

9

Post-Call Positive

Dr. Kahn was wearing street clothes in the hospital lobby. Dr. Linton, in on-call whites, appeared at her heels. Sima stood alongside them with a patient in a wheelchair under her charge.

Elevator Lady Miss Lawrence focused her eyes on the patient. "Where you headed with her, Sima?"

"A71."

Sima maneuvered the wheelchair and IV pole to face the front of the operator-controlled transport box where she spent so much time, situated hindmost to make room for others. Dr. Kahn and Dr. Linton faced forward, their backs walling her off. Miss Lawrence's queenly digit let go of the OPEN button. The door closed them in.

Dr. Linton stood by Miss Lawrence, his clipboard resting on the ledge of his belt. It was an Indian summer in New York City, and he wore short sleeves and a dark-blue tie Sima liked. He wasn't wearing his short white intern's jacket. Stethoscope flung around his neck, tourniquet knotted through a loop on his belt, note cards neatly clipped in his shirt pocket. His arm muscled down to strong fingers curled over the top of the clipboard. Picture-perfect male intern, primed for performance, day and night.

Miss Lawrence eyed Dr. Linton as he flipped through lab slips attached to his to-do list. "Quite a list you got there," she said.

"A good intern knows how to take care of *all* the patients on the ward." He tapped his clipboard with his pen, *tap, tap*, placed the pen behind his ear, and then pulled it out again. *Tap, tap, tap.* He glanced to his right at Dr. Kahn.

Dr. Kahn didn't acknowledge his bearing. She rocked on her heels, the knee-length hem of her black A-line skirt self-consciously showing her slim legs, stocking-less and untanned.

"Strep faecalis," Dr. Linton said. He dangled a lab report in front of Dr. Kahn. "One of my patient's blood cultures came back positive. One out of three."

Strep faecalis was one of the contaminants Sima heard the interns talk about. Dr. Kahn had gone through with it. She had taken blood from Miss Osborn's groin. Sima scrutinized Dr. Kahn's face perusing the evidence.

Miss Lawrence reached from her chair and snatched the slip from Dr. Kahn's hand. "We got a patient in here. *No* doctor talk."

Dr. Linton retrieved the slip and tucked it with his others. All passengers faced the elevator door. No eye contact. The fan at the back blew stuffy air over everyone's head.

A few minutes later, Dr. Linton cleared his throat. Without facing his colleague, he said to her, "Did you do a femoral stick two nights ago?"

"No," Dr. Kahn said, without hesitation.

The elevator door opened. Miss Lawrence raised her voice but didn't shout. "Take your talk out of my elevator."

Before Sima could roll her patient out, Dr. Kahn was halfway down the hall. Dr. Linton marched after her. The psych rotator had lied and Sima knew it. She was disappointed to see Dr. Kahn run off like that.

SIMA SITUATED THE PATIENT IN her charge in bed, unlocked the wheelchair, and was about to walk away when the woman asked her to cover her legs. Sima slammed the chair against the bed and complied without a word.

"What's the matter with you?" Alma Mae squeaked from the next bed. She patted the blanket on her bed. "Come here, child."

Sima wasn't in the mood for a chat, but Alma Mae reached her bony fingers out, grabbing hold of her arm where she stood between the two beds.

"So tell me," Alma Mae said. "I know you're working on that last course of yours."

"I'm not working on anything," Sima said.

"You already told me you were," Alma Mae said.

Sima had told Alma Mae she needed to take English composition to graduate but she hadn't told her she'd decided not to register for the course, never mind drop out altogether.

Alma Mae coughed. "You can talk to me. I'm not your prying mother, in case you haven't noticed."

Sima couldn't hide her smile at the thought of the two women fighting over her. Her mother would refuse to talk with a *shvartze*, a black, even if her mother spoke English, even if the *shvartze* only weighed eighty pounds and her mother weighed a hundred and eighty. She'd act as if the tiny woman could kill her with her cough. Sima sat down in the wheelchair and stared at the swirly linoleum floor.

"So?" Alma Mae said, as if she were the Jewish one in the room.

"Remember the other night with Miss Osborn?" Sima spoke quietly. It wasn't like her to gossip. And Miss Osborn was still in the hospital. She'd been moved to the Isolation

Room until they could figure out the cause of her fever and diarrhea.

"That pooping fatso—who could forget her?" Alma Mae said.

"It's not about her," Sima said. "It's about Dr. Kahn."

"What can you say about that one?" Alma said. "She's a wannabe. What'd she do?"

"She lied," Sima whispered.

"So what? Everybody lies." Alma Mae spoke with authority and forgiveness.

"I don't lie." She shuffled her feet on the floor, moving the wheelchair forward and back.

"Oh, you're so proper and good. You don't ever do nothing wrong. I'm so proud of you."

"I'm not perfect," Sima said.

"Well, neither is she," Alma Mae said. "So stop making a fuss about it. What did she lie about you can't tell me?"

Sima ran her thumb along the armrest of the chair, feeling for blemishes. If she told Alma Mae, then what? Who else would she have to tell? But was what Dr. Kahn did really such a big deal? Dr. Linton knew, everyone else would too. It was just evidence Dr. Kahn wasn't cut out to be a medical intern. She was only rotating through Medicine because it was required for Psychiatry. Not so different from having to pass English composition.

AT THE DOUBLE DOOR TO the open ward, the intern team on A71 milled around. Their senior resident was late for work rounds again. Dr. Kahn was juggling three charts. One slammed to the floor. Dr. Kahn bent down to retrieve it.

As Dr. Kahn stood up, Sima bumped elbows with her. She tapped the top of the chart rack to get the team's attention. She'd seen Chief Danielson do that. He'd told her she might be Chief material one day.

"Miss Potter says you guys have to discharge somebody. I just brought up the first hit, and there aren't any beds," Sima said. The house staff called new admissions *hits*. Post-call, they bragged about how many they'd had. Proof they'd been hard hit by enemy fire and survived. Sima liked to use this insider's word, to use any insider word she understood which was most of them.

"Why do they send up a patient if we don't have beds?" Dr. Linton said. "This place is so disorganized." Dr. Linton, handsome and organized, kept an inventory of mismanaged orders, out-of-stock supplies, under-supported services, and the extra hours of pointless work these deficiencies created for interns.

"So what does your Chiefness suggest we do about it?" Dr. Long said. The balding ex-surgery intern twisted his thick blond mustache. He was the one dressed in on-call whites.

"Alma Mae's been ready to go for days," Dr. Linton said. He pulled Alma's chart from the rack and placed it on top. "Dr. Kahn can discharge her before rounds."

"I have to clear it with Miguel," Dr. Kahn said. "He's the senior."

"His judgment's worse than a medical student's," Dr. Linton said.

"Mindy's a psych rotator," Dr. Long said. "Give her a break."

"And you're an ex-surgery intern," Dr. Linton said. "What do you know?"

Sima was surprised to hear Dr. Long stand up for Dr. Kahn. And then Steinberg, a head shorter than both Long and Linton, spoke. "Dr. Kahn is better than most medical interns."

"You always stick up for your own kind," Dr. Long said.

"And what is 'my own kind'?" Steinberg crossed his arms over his chest. He pushed his horn rims up on his nose, like a college professor. After his year on Medicine, he was headed for Ophthalmology, one of the most competitive specialties.

"One of the yarmulke boys," Dr. Long chuckled.

"Steinberg doesn't wear a yarmulke," Dr. Kahn said, one decibel louder than usual.

Steinberg adjusted his glasses again. "And I don't worm

my way out of call Friday nights and Saturdays to go to synagogue like they do either. I pull my weight around here, and so does Dr. Kahn."

Dr. Kahn leaned into Steinberg. "You don't have to defend me."

"No, he doesn't." Dr. Linton motioned to Dr. Kahn. "Can I talk with you a minute?" He backed away from the chart rack and put his hands on his hips. Sima didn't like this male doctor insider stance—*I know what's what, and you better listen up if you know what's good for you.* Dr. Linton might be the best medical intern on the team, but he was still only a few months out of medical school like the rest of them.

Dr. Kahn armored Alma Mae's chart tight to her chest and stepped toward Dr. Linton for their private conversation, but everyone was close enough to hear.

"Just make sure all the IVs are back in by work rounds the next time you're on," he said. "Including Miss Osborn's."

Dr. Kahn stretched her long neck out of her blouse like a turtle peeking out to face a predator. "Every patient whose IV was out got antibiotics if they needed them," she said. "IM and on time."

"We all have bad nights." Dr. Linton faced her directly. "But when Long or Steinberg have one, I don't have to stay late the next day to finish what they didn't do."

"Half the IVs on the ward were out that night. I was there," Sima said. It *had* been a hard call for Dr. Kahn. Sima knew—it had been a horrible double shift for her, too.

Steinberg clapped, Dr. Long patted her on the back. It wasn't like Sima to speak up.

"Thank you, Dr. Sima. But this is not an orderly issue." Dr. Linton had spoken.

And so had Sima.

Part Two

10

Train Wrecks

Mrs. Sampson had been in and out of the hospital every three weeks for breast cancer. Sima had watched from a distance as interns struggled to replace her IVs, no easier than with the addicts. It was clear to her that getting stuck for chemo wasn't much better for a person's veins than sticking them for street powder. In the end, shot-up veins were shot-up veins. And what was left of the woman's hair from chemo jutted straight out the top of her red-and-white bandana.

"Mrs. Sampson," she said, "your doctor ordered a chest X-ray for you."

The old woman wore glasses attached to a rope that hung from her neck. A small plaid shirt—green, red, and yellow—lay over her white-sheeted knees, a metal thimble covered the end of the middle finger of her sewing hand. Mrs. Sampson tugged at a dark thread, wrapped it around a finger, and yanked until the thread broke off. She pulled a spool out of her bathrobe pocket and unrolled another long piece.

"You should meet my little grandson, Sammy," Mrs. Sampson said as if Sima had just joined her sewing circle. She poked the thread into the eye of the needle and pulled it through. "We hardly ever see his mama. My other daughter is raising him. They all live with me."

Sima thrummed a wheelchair back. "We don't have much time to get you downstairs."

Mrs. Sampson squinted at Sima over the top of her glasses. "You're just like Sammy's mother—and every young person I meet. Always needing to dash."

"I'm just doing my job." Sima folded her arms over her scrubs shirt.

Mrs. Sampson straightened her bathrobe. One side of her chest was flat; Sima presumed a missing breast. "Bring that wheelchair over here."

Sima maneuvered the wheelchair against the side of the bed and set the brake. Mrs. Sampson threw the bed sheet off and swung her naked, bony knees over the side.

"Hand me them slippers," she said. "Can't stand on these floors in my bare feet, Sima."

Sima handed Mrs. Sampson her pink fuzzy slippers and clicked her heels. "Orderly Sima," she said.

"At ease, private," Mrs. Sampson said. "This ain't no army."

Mrs. Sampson grabbed onto Sima's arm with one hand and held the back of her robe against her bottom with the other. She stood facing the wall, her backside to Sima, and then eased herself down into the wheelchair.

"Please cover my knees," she said.

Patients always asked to be covered. Sima dropped a blanket onto the old woman's lap.

"And hand me my sewing," Mrs. Sampson said. "They always keep me an hour or two." The old woman opened the blanket and smoothed it over her legs. "All those moaning sick folk in X-ray talk you to death about how the neighborhood's all gangs and hoodlums. The streets never been safe." She waved at the plaid shirt left crumpled in the middle of the bed, attached to her thread and needle, and as Sima reached for it, she said, "Be careful of the needle."

Sima had seen needles all over the County, from her first day there. Doctors got hepatitis from accidental sticks, or when they got too busy or lazy and didn't bother to put on gloves. It was easier to feel for a vein without the rubber layer between skin. And now there was the new blood-borne illness. Infectious disease specialists wandered the wards, ordering interns to glove up every at blood draw like never before. And even though they wore masks with

TB patients on a closed ward, doctors got sick every year. Orderlies were vulnerable, but no one seemed to worry about orderlies.

Sima worked at the County because it was only four subway stops from where she lived and she could work nights, and could go another four stops to college during the day. Since there were no private doctors, interns and residents could run the wards and the ER, thrilled to be in charge, while still in training. She wondered why patients came to the County. Patients didn't know they could go to any hospital with an ER, even a fancy one on the Upper East Side. Sima figured people in Brooklyn stayed with their own when they got sick. She was sure her mother would go to Coney Island Hospital with the Russian Jews.

Sima watched Mrs. Sampson use her thimble finger carefully to locate the needle wedged in the small plaid shirt.

"My father was a tailor," Sima said. "But he had to sweep floors at my school. The Poles didn't want Jews touching their clothes."

Mrs. Sampson wrinkled her forehead. "Too bad. Tailoring is good work."

THE SOUND OF THE ELEVATOR door closing was followed by a faint, tinny noise. Miss Lawrence leaned over from her chair and picked up Mrs. Sampson's thimble.

"My mama had one of these." Miss Lawrence put it on her index finger.

"The thimble finger is the *middle* finger," Mrs. Sampson said.

"Can I hold it?" Sima said.

Miss Lawrence twisted the thimble off her chunky digit. She raised her hand up for Sima to take the tiny silvery cup.

Sima placed the thimble on.

"It fits," Miss Lawrence said.

"It fits all lady fingers," Mrs. Sampson said.

"Maybe you have a calling outside these here walls, Sima," Miss Lawrence said.

That wasn't a thought Sima was ready to consider. She'd been taking pre-med courses for so long now and yet it seemed impossible to think of herself as one of the doctors. She was more comfortable being an orderly.

Miss Lawrence opened the elevator door on the third floor, and there was Dr. Kahn. Sima hadn't seen her in a few weeks, not since she'd stood up to Dr. Linton on her behalf. Dr. Kahn stepped inside, her clipboard to her chest. Sima started to smile at her but Dr. Kahn stood stiffly, staring straight ahead, and Sima recalled the intern's lie.

Miss Lawrence pushed one of her control buttons and the elevator door closed.

"They need me upstairs," Dr. Kahn said.

"It's good to be needed," Mrs. Sampson beamed at Dr. Kahn as she lifted Sammy's small shirt from her lap. She shook out the wrinkles and then lay the shirt button-side down, with the little short sleeves hanging over the sides of her knees.

"My mother took in sewing in Poland," Sima said. She still fingered the thimble, now warm against her skin the way her mother's thimble had been when she darned socks.

"Neighborly," Miss Lawrence said.

"Poles hated Jewish neighbors," Sima said. "My mother only sewed for Jews."

It wasn't just that Sima's father couldn't work as a tailor because he was a Jew. After a while, he couldn't work at all. After the doctor told him he shouldn't shovel snow because of his heart. He lay on the sofa, his swollen feet curled up under the blue blanket her mother knit for him. He spent his days searching the newspaper for the comic strip that still featured Polish police standing over a Jew long after the war, the cartoons he instructed Sima to save for his file.

"I guess living in New York is better," Mrs. Sampson said.

Dr. Kahn looked at Sima now. "In New York, no one ever asks me if I have Jewish hair."

Sima kept her gaze on Dr. Kahn. "In New York, no one calls me a *brudny zyd*."

That's what a girl called her once, only once, in Poland. It was spring, the week before Easter, and the snow was melting. The willow tree in front of her house was sprinkled with green buds. It was the mean girl from the end of the street, the one with curly, dark hair, even though she wasn't Jewish. Sima knew the girl hated her own hair. She was always trying new ways to tie it back or cover it up. Bows, ribbons, scarves, hats. She was a head shorter than Sima. She was older and wiser, she said, because she was seven. And it didn't matter that Sima was taller because Sima was a *brudny zyd*. A dirty Jew. The girl told Sima she could scrub her face, her arms, and her legs all day and night, but she would never be clean. She'd always be *brudny*. Dirty. Sima's mother told her words like that could only come from the girl's father or her mother. No seven-year-old could come up with anything so nasty. Sima should feel sorry for the girl, her mother said. It wasn't her fault she spoke such horrible words. But Sima didn't know how to feel sorry for her.

Sima still wasn't sure what she should feel about Dr. Kahn's lie.

AFTER THE X-RAY WAS TAKEN, Sima delivered Mrs. Sampson back to the Nurses' Station. Another woman patient sat there in a wheelchair. She was big boned and had hair to her shoulders styled in a stiff flip. Fire-engine red lipstick and matching three-inch fingernails. One high, black cheekbone was swollen and bore a bruise the color of an eggplant, and a slash closed with tiny black stitches crossed the laugh lines in her forehead. Her shapely legs were crossed, top foot bouncing off the bottom foot. She strummed her goosey neck with one hand and held her hospital johnny closed at the crotch with the other hand. The crotch hand clutched her admitting papers.

"Long night," she said in a throaty voice to Mrs. Sampson.

Mrs. Sampson snugged her blanket around her legs, the spool of thread and scissors atop the plaid button-down in her lap. "Hmmm."

"So how old are you?" Miss Bingham, the night nurse, asked in her cigarette-boozy voice.

"Only time will tell how old I am. At night, light and time are on *my* side."

Nurse Bingham tapped her purpled pen on her vital-signs chart. "I need to know your age."

"Name's Brandy, hon." She raised her papers in the air. "Can I go to my room now?"

"This ain't no hotel, Brandy, dear. You have to see the doctor first." Nurse Bingham lifted the papers from Brandy's hand, ran her pen down the front sheet. "Twenty-one?" she chuckled. "You and me both, sweetheart."

"I didn't come to the hospital to be insulted." Brandy tightened the cross of her legs, her hand, now without the papers, back in her crotch.

Dr. Kahn walked toward them.

"Mrs. Sampson's back from X-ray," Sima said to her.

Dr. Kahn nodded. She took Brandy's chart from Nurse Bingham and slipped it into the pocket on the back of her wheelchair. She kicked the brake lever and started down the hallway, Sima trailing with Mrs. Sampson in her chair, back to the Female Room, the six-bedded suite for A71 ladies, where Mrs. Sampson would now have one more roommate.

WHEN THE SECOND HALF OF her double shift began, Sima had been up most of the night but hadn't seen much of Dr. Kahn. Sima had nodded off briefly in a geri chair in the Doctors' Charting Room. Now she could hear the doctors' voices outside the room as they huddled around the chart rack to start work rounds. She got up from the chair, peered into a mirror on one of the doctors' lockers, to settle her hair. She stepped out into the hallway and saw Dr. Kahn holding an X-ray up to the light.

Just then, a scream issued from the female bathroom a few feet away.

Dr. Kahn and Sima were closest. Sima pushed on the

door, but it would open only a crack. She squeezed through and held the door so Dr. Kahn could follow. Bump-stop to the door, preventing it from fully opening, were pink fuzzy slippers on old lady feet. Stationed over the fallen body was Brandy. She had one foot in the sink and her blue johnny flung behind her neck like a cape. Two perfect round-as-round-can-be breasts shone watery in the light. And then there was the part that must have been the cause of the screaming and fainting: Brandy had a penis.

Miss Armstrong, head nurse that day, was trying to see what was going on. Since the door wouldn't open fully and she was too big to squeeze through, she could only get her face into the room. "Who's that down on the floor?"

"Mrs. Sampson," Sima said. She squatted on the floor by the old lady and found her chin inches from Brandy's crotch. The penis was wrinkly, soft, the tip hooded—the only uncircumcised one she'd seen other than her baby brother's before the ritual ceremony. She had a ridiculous urge to reach out and touch it.

Brandy folded herself deeper into the sink, soaping her legs, right down to the perfect red toenails. She looked like a dancer stretching, in a position no one else in the room could have dreamed of holding. Water trickled from the faucet and mixed with the suds on the smooth, black skin—face, breasts, crotch. It dripped down the tip of the penis onto Mrs. Sampson's slippers.

"What are you doing in there?" Miss Armstrong said in her megaphone voice the ward team behind her could hear.

"A girl's got to stay clean." Brandy smiled.

"First things first," Miss Armstrong said.

Sima felt Mrs. Sampson's wrist, the way she'd seen the doctors do. "I can feel her pulse."

Dr. Kahn managed to reach down, confirmed. Sima was pleased with herself.

"Dr. Kahn, Sima," Miss Armstrong said, still strongholding the side of the door open for a bird's-eye view. "Get Mrs. Sampson out of here." She squeezed one arm into the room and pointed at Brandy. "And you missy, mister— you'll finish cleaning up in your room."

Sima and Dr. Kahn cradled Mrs. Sampson's head and back and raised her to sitting. Mrs. Sampson's pink-slippered feet and bony legs were no longer blocking the entrance. Miss Armstrong removed her head and arm from the room and opened the door to get the full picture. And now standing behind her was the A71 intern team. They were bunched like a bouquet of flowers, bodies pressed together like stems, faces turned toward the open entry as if it were the sun.

Miss Armstrong widened her eyes at Dr. Kahn but spoke to the others. "Seems the intern on-call forgot to tell us a thing or two about one of our new patients here."

THE DOCTORS' CHARTING ROOM WAS a mess of white-coated bodies. Brandy's X-ray was up on the view box. The bones of her skull showed in silhouette against the light, and all eyes in the room were staring at those bones.

Sima leaned against the door, trying to hide behind Miss Armstrong while she listened in. Dr. Kahn hid behind the rest of the team. Her wire rims were crooked on her face, her post-call hairdo not much better than Sima's.

Miss Armstrong pushed her way to the middle of the group. "So why didn't we know our Brandy is not who she says she is, Dr. Kahn?" She turned to the psych-rotator extraordinaire. "You didn't think it would be a good idea to tell us the old girl had another tool for her trade?"

Dr. Steinberg switched off the view box. "You just put it all down in your incident report, Miss Armstrong." He had a big smirk on his face. "We'll take care of the rest."

"Incident report!" Miss Armstrong folded her arms atop her white polyester bosom. Nobody messed with Miss Armstrong the way nobody messed with Miss Lawrence. "What we got here is more than an Incident Report," she said. "Dr. Kahn is just lucky the County's not one of them swanky white people's hospitals, or you'd have lawyers all over the place."

Dr. Steinberg flipped the switch of the view box again, on, then off, then on.

Dr. Linton stepped in front of him. "Will you stop that?"

Sima poked her nose in from behind Miss Armstrong. "Does Mrs. Sampson need an X-ray? I can take her," she said. She wanted to get a jump start before Miss Armstrong could attack Dr. Kahn another time. Sima surprised herself, trying again to protect this floundering wannabe who could pass for her sister when they were both cleaned up. Dr. Kahn might be on the verge of messing up her career and some part of Sima wanted to be her friend, no matter what.

11

Brooklyn–Battery Tunnel

It was the week after Thanksgiving. An early-season snow had closed the schools and stranded staff in the hospital. Two in the morning and Sima walked into the Doctors' Charting Room. Steam from the clunky radiator under the window hissed into the air the way it did in every old New York City building she had ever been in. She saw Dr. Kahn sitting at the counter. Her hair, attacked by the steam, was frizzed out even in the dead of this early winter pre-dawn. Her white jacket was draped over the back of her chair, and as much skin was exposed as her on-call outfit would allow. Sleeves of a black turtleneck under her scrubs shirt were pushed up to her elbows; the legs of her scrubs pants were rolled above her knees. She was leaning forward almost off the seat of a chair. Her left hand rested on the telephone receiver, her right in the middle of an open chart. She stared at the wall in front of her.

"You can turn off the radiator in here, you know," Sima said.

Dr. Kahn lowered her eyes to the chart pages and sat back in the chair.

Sima started toward the radiator, and then she heard the scrape of chair legs behind her.

"My father's wife just called," Dr. Kahn said.

"Your father's wife?" Sima said.

"My parents are divorced," she said. "My father lives in Manhattan. He's remarried."

"It's two o'clock in the morning."

"She said he hasn't moved his car in three days."

"Lots of cars haven't moved in all this snow," Sima said.

"They're separated and she walks by their building every day." Dr. Kahn passed a hand across her sweaty forehead and then wiped it on the leg of her scrub pants. "There are parking tickets all over the windshield. He never leaves parking tickets on his car."

"She can see them with all this snow?"

Dr. Kahn didn't answer.

Sima hardly knew anyone who drove beside the doctors at the County, but everyone knew about alternate-side-of-the-street parking and how easy it was to get parking tickets. Monday/Wednesday/Friday or Tuesday/Thursday/Saturday, 8 a.m. to 11 a.m. or 11 a.m. to 2 p.m. She'd seen people sitting in their cars reading the paper, waiting until it was time to move to the other side. One New York City ritual those without a car didn't envy.

"Maybe he's out of town." Sima didn't know what to say.

"He never goes out of town." Dr. Kahn pulled the black sleeves down to her wrists and stood up. She lifted her white jacket off the back of the chair and began to put it on. With one sleeve partly on, she suddenly sat down again, and the rest of the jacket drooped onto the floor.

Sima stepped over to rescue the jacket. "This floor is gross," she said. The soles of her running shoes stuck to the linoleum. The jacket slipped into Sima's hand without any resistance from Dr. Kahn. Sima sat down nearby, draped the jacket over her lap, trying to keep anything from falling out of the pockets. "What's wrong?"

"She wants me to go to his apartment to check on him."

"Why doesn't she go?"

"She called, she rang the bell—he doesn't answer," Dr. Kahn said.

The steam from the radiator hissed and spat. Sima sat quietly alongside Dr. Kahn.

The intern stared down at her salt-stained running shoes. In a tiny voice, as if she were a child afraid to go to the bathroom in the dark, she said to Sima, "Will you go with me?"

Sima had never been with Dr. Kahn anywhere outside the hospital. Two in the morning in the middle of a snowstorm.

"OK," she said.

EVERY CAR IN THE COUNTY parking lot was covered with snow. Dr. Kahn pulled a brush from the trunk of her car to clean the driver's side windshield. She handed the brush to Sima to get the passenger's side. Then she leaned into the car and stretched her arm to clear the roof in one big sweep, the back window in another. Sima could see Dr. Kahn had experience with snow. There was a trail of it down the front of her heavy winter coat.

The car was so close to a drift on the passenger's side that Sima couldn't open the door. She had to get in on the driver's side. She squeezed under the steering wheel and inched her way across the front seat. She'd only ridden in a taxicab a few times in New York and a truck once or twice as a child in Poland; no one she knew there had a car. She watched the large flakes land on the windshield under the glow of the streetlight.

"Is it safe to drive?" Sima said.

Dr. Kahn turned the key in the ignition. "I've got snow tires."

In the dark, the heaps of snow looked like photographs of the North Pole Sima had seen in *National Geographic*. Except for the bits of red-brick buildings, the roofs of cars, telephone poles, streetlights. Her toes were getting cold. She had been caught by the snowstorm without winter boots, same as Dr. Kahn. She rubbed her gloved hands together.

"The heater takes a while to get going. This old Rambler Rebel is almost as old as we are—my first and only car," Dr. Kahn said. "I bought it from a little old lady in Massachusetts." Medical student loans. That was all she could afford.

The car moved slowly down side streets. Sima held tightly to the armrest; she didn't ask any questions. She didn't want to distract Dr. Kahn.

"Flatbush Avenue should be OK," Dr. Kahn said. She turned right, skidding slightly onto the wider street.

In the quiet of the Rebel, they headed down the long avenue that crossed the borough on a diagonal toward the Brooklyn Bridge, past closed-up storefronts: a coffee shop on almost every corner, several newsstands, a shoe repair, a CVS Pharmacy, a branch of Citibank, a Safeway, a hardware store. The usual Brooklyn litter—bits of tossed paper, soda cans and abandoned bottles, a solitary glove—was buried by snow; the streets looked clean. White, unblemished. Sima loved the look of new snow even in the dark, in a storm. Snowflakes falling under the streetlights. It reminded her of winters in Poland and building snowmen with her father before he got sick.

A snowplow blocked the entrance to the Brooklyn Bridge. A sign posted a detour to the Brooklyn–Battery Tunnel.

"Damn," Dr. Kahn said. The car skidded again as she turned around and headed toward the tunnel several blocks away. Sima held on, her first ride in a private car.

They were getting out of Brooklyn—the same way as to get out of any of the boroughs that wasn't Manhattan, or out of New Jersey, through a tunnel or over a bridge or on a subway train. Bridge and tunnel people—what New Yorkers called those like Sima who had the bad luck to live so far from the center of the universe. It was like that *New Yorker* magazine cover she had seen on the bulletin board at Brooklyn College, with Manhattan at the center and the rest of America on the other side of the Hudson.

The Rebel nosed up alongside the tollbooth. A sliding window opened and ash flicked out. Tollbooth Guy: surprising in the snowstorm to see his cheeks puff out, a cloud of gray exhaled into the winter white. When she was five, Sima had loved to watch her father's smoke rings come out of his mouth and disappear into the sky. He taught her to count them.

"You young ladies shouldn't be driving in a storm at this hour."

Dr. Kahn put her hand out with three dollar bills for the $2.50 toll. She pressed the money into his hand and rolled up her window.

"Hey?" Tollbooth Guy knocked on the car roof.

The signal light flashed green and Dr. Kahn drove fast into the tunnel.

"You didn't get your change," Sima said.

Dr. Kahn kept her foot on the gas.

In the middle of the night, only one leg of the tunnel was open. It was two-way single file. Bright lights shone every thirty feet or so, six feet up on both walls. In between the lights, there were dark shadows and the headlights of the Rebel. The driver's side tire hugged the center line, on the yellow brick road into Mayor Koch's Big Apple. A car in the opposite lane flashed its brights and for a few seconds blinded them. Sima closed her eyes and then rubbed them open.

"I hate this drive," Dr. Kahn said. "My father never drives in tunnels. The bad air gives him chest pain." She gripped the steering wheel harder, leaned forward on the seat, as if that could make the car move faster.

A bulb on the tunnel wall was out, and there were places under the lights where water dripped down, as if the river were leaking through. Sima had to stop herself from thinking about all that river water. The tunnel was all around them. Overhead, the Staten Island Ferry, only twenty-five cents one way, and the boat to Ellis Island where Aunt Miriam had cleared immigration twenty-five years ago, not at all like the way Sima and her mother had come, through JFK. And just a few blocks up the West Side Highway, on the other end of the tunnel, Wall Street and bankers' fancy apartment buildings.

THEY TURNED OFF AT THE Seventy-Ninth Street Boat Basin and slowed down by a fenced-in area.

"I played tennis here with my father a few weeks ago," Dr. Kahn said. "It was still warm. The City hadn't taken down the nets yet."

"He can't drive through tunnels, but he can play tennis?" Sima asked.

"It's all about oxygen," she said. "Not enough of it in tunnel air. He can play guys in their thirties—he makes them run for balls."

At West Seventy-First Street, there was a red light and only one other car on the road, a Checker cab in front of them with its right turn signal on. Dr. Kahn hit the horn. "Turn, you asshole!"

Sima had never heard Dr. Kahn talk like that.

"It's 3:00 a.m., and we're going to my father's apartment,"

she shouted. "My father's wife has *never* called me. Why would she call me in the middle of a damn snowstorm?"

"Did she say your father was sick?"

"Nothing. She said nothing."

Sima thought Dr. Kahn might say, "It doesn't look good," what she often heard doctors say to a family member when their loved one had taken a turn for the worse, or had already died. She figured that was why Dr. Kahn was so jumpy. Neither of them was going to say it out loud.

Dr. Kahn pulled up alongside a car with parking tickets sticking out of the snow. She put her warning signals on and got out of the car, double parked. She brushed the snow off the driver's side, cupped her hands to the windows; Sima was at her elbow and saw on the passenger seat the *Times* movie pages and a half-eaten pastrami on rye, dried mustard on the outside edges.

"Tunnels and pastrami," Dr. Kahn said. "He said they'd kill him."

DR. KAHN STOOD IN FRONT OF the door to her father's apartment, bits of snow falling off her coat onto the floor. Sima could see the intern's glasses had fogged up. She pulled a tissue from her coat pocket and handed it to her. Dr. Kahn didn't remove her glasses, snuck the tissue in behind each lens and swiped it. She didn't push the doorbell or knock. She raised the hand with the tissue to the peephole in the door and wiped the peephole too.

"My father paneled all the walls in his apartment and put up wooden blinds. He's a cave dweller who grows roses in his backyard, if you can call it that."

Gardens bloom in the dark. Three-by-five rectangles of city soil, dug up and watered and seeded and pruned. Standing gardens hiding in between the backs of five-story walk-ups, stretching their stems and thorns and leaves and petals up to reach the light as it reaches down and passes over back-to-back rectangles behind the side-by-side brick boxes that Manhattanites call home. Nothing grew at the back of Sima's ten-story Brooklyn building; there was nothing there but cement and a few broken window screens lying on the ground.

Sima stood alongside Dr. Kahn and ran a gloved finger down the doorpost. "There's no mezuzah," she said. The small box that held a scroll of the Jewish prayer, the *Shema*. Every Jew hung one on the front door. "Jews were afraid to put up mezuzahs in Poland after the war."

"Something happened to my father during the war," Dr. Kahn said. "And then in the '50s, McCarthyism. He got stuck there—he thinks everyone's either a Commie pinko or a Jew hater."

"My father wanted to join the army. But they wouldn't take Jews," Sima said. "Papa said, 'Jews don't go to war.

That's Jewish history, back to the days of the Babylonians. Wherever they are, the war comes to the Jews.'" Sima didn't remember her father saying this but her mother had repeated her father's statement so many times.

"The first time my mother let me spend the High Holidays with my father here," Dr. Kahn said, "I wanted to go to the synagogue. I'd never missed Yom Kippur services. My father said it was good for me not to go once, so I'd know the world wouldn't come to an end."

"My aunt keeps pushing me to go to services to meet a Jewish man, a doctor," Sima said. "But I don't want to marry a doctor, I want to be one." Sima had never said this out loud before to anyone other than Alma Mae. She hoped Dr. Kahn had been too distracted to hear it.

Dr. Kahn didn't budge. She fingered the peephole again. "My father has a blue sofa and a blue shag rug. Remember those ugly things from the '60s?"

Sima shrugged. "I was in Poland until 1966."

Dr. Kahn stepped back from the door, and when Sima turned around, she was sitting down on the stairs to the second floor. She removed her gloves, then took off her wire rims and made another effort to wipe them. Then she set the gloves and glasses down on the step.

"I don't want to go in there," she said.

Middle of the night. No screeching bus wheels. No car horns or alarms. Just quiet.

Dr. Kahn unwound her scarf and unbuttoned her coat. Sima sat down alongside her.

"He has a blue bathrobe and three blue velour shirts. Blue is my mother's favorite color." Dr. Kahn cleared her throat. "They've been divorced now longer than they were married."

Blue like the family heirloom glass Sima's father held on to, passed down from his great grandmother. Her mother sold it right after he died so they could go to America.

Sima pulled off her hat and gloves and held them in her lap. There was a snowy line of footprints from the door of the building to the door of the apartment, and now to the steps where she sat with Dr. Kahn.

"This year I've seen my father every two weeks," Dr. Kahn said, "since the start of internship. We go out for Chinese food and a movie. It's all I can do without falling asleep."

Dr. Kahn put her glasses on. She stood up. She rang the buzzer by the apartment door.

A short woman opened the door, the top of her head even with Dr. Kahn's nose. To Sima, she looked like the blonde on Aunt Miriam's Clairol box. She had the kind of hair fingers got stuck in, the look of chubby women from Brooklyn or Queens trying to be Manhattan chic. Middle of the night and the woman's hair was poofy, her eyelashes long, thick, black, American movie-star lashes. Aunt Miriam sent her mother posters of American movies. Her mother wanted to go to America but she hated those posters as much as her father did.

"You're here," was all the blond woman said. She turned away from them. As she walked, her backside jiggled through black slinky pants.

To the left inside the door was a wall of books, ceiling to floor—paperbacks and hardcovers, some not quite straight on the shelves. There on one of the shelves, a black-and-white photograph of a couple. He had dark hair, dark glasses, a suit and tie, his hand was over hers and they were holding a knife, about to cut a cake. The woman was the blonde with the poofy hair and black lashes. They were both smiling.

Sima saw the blue sofa against the back wall of the living room and the matching blue shag rug on which a police officer stood, her hat in her hands. "Are you the daughter?" she said.

"Where's my father?" Dr. Kahn said.

"I'm sorry," the police office said. "Your mother called us."

"She's not my mother." Dr. Kahn pushed between them into the hallway that led to the bedroom. Bits of snow flaked off her coat onto the blue shag rug.

There was a mezuzah on the bedroom doorpost, silver with bits of blue stone. Sima raised her hand toward Dr. Kahn's snow-flecked shoulder. Dr. Kahn fingered the mezuzah and stepped over the threshold. The tails of her scarf made a wavy shadow against the door. Sima followed. The room smelled of piss and shit. There was a triangle of light coming in through the open door, just enough to see skin: the soles of two feet sticking out from under the sheets and blanket.

Dr. Kahn reached back toward Sima now, catching her hand and squeezing it. With her other hand she touched the heel of her father's foot. She lifted the corner of the sheet and placed it back down carefully on top of his ankles.

"Sheets make my father's feet hurt, he never covers them," Dr. Kahn said. His face was turned to one side, away from them, so quiet.

Her own father's face—Sima had seen it, on its side. His eyes were closed. Sima had found him, on the floor of his study. Thick black-gray eyebrow scrunched up above her eye, the one she could see. His mouth, his blue lips. Sima hardly remembered more than her father's face and the way he lay there, the silence. She remembered the whole room as Dr. Kahn now would, the almost-closed wooden blinds, the light coming through the doorway, illuminating her father's naked feet.

12

Death Note

Sima pushed an empty stretcher into the Cardiac Care Unit. She had never seen Miss Armstrong work in the CCU but there she was that night, her hand on the wrist of a white man sitting up in the bed closest to the Nurses' Station. He was barrel-chested and hairy—a semicircle of white hair a crown on his balding head, curlicues of it out the neck of his hospital gown and down his arms. In her four years as an orderly at the sprawling Brooklyn hospital and the only immigrant there who didn't hail from a Caribbean island, Sima had never seen such a patient at the County. Alongside Miss Armstrong's Jamaican black, the man looked as if all the blood and pigment had been drained out of him.

"Give a hand here, Sima."

With her left hip, Sima lodged her stretcher up against the wall nearest the door to the CCU and set the brake, all the time with her eyes on the pale man. She approached the nearest side of the bed, opposite Miss Armstrong.

This patient may have been different than their usual, but they had stood alongside hospital bedrails more times than either of them could count. They steadied their hands and forearms under the large man's upper arms. On the count of three, they tried to maneuver his body up against the raised pillow behind him. Eyes wide and bloodshot, the old man stared straight ahead. He grabbed the rails as though he were in a boat about to tip. He shook the rails and wouldn't let go.

"He's sure to pull out that IV," Miss Armstrong huffed. She lifted the IV bag off its pole to untwist the tubing and then hung it back on its perch.

Sima eyed the name on the man's wrist band.

"*Siedziec prosto*," she said to him in Polish, her native language. Sit up.

Miss Armstrong nudged Sima. "One of *your* people?"

Sima searched for and found an Eastern Orthodox cross around the man's neck. Slavic, Ukrainian. She felt for the gold six-pointed Jewish star under the edge of her scrubs shirt. *Not* one of *her* people. Her ears got hot. Here in America, in New York, New York, a simple, uneducated Polish Jewish peasant immigrant could become someone with the upper hand, someone this man could never harm, and a Caribbean woman's touch held his life on the line.

The man grunted. He let go of the bed rails and

wrapped his arms around his barrel chest. "Tell him he'll more comfortable if he sits against the pillow," Miss Armstrong said.

"*Siedziec prosto,*" Sima said again. "*Bedziesz bardziej wygodne.*" Sit up. You'll be more comfortable.

Sima's face was now inches from the man's, close to the deep folds that led from his nose to the corners of his mouth. His lips were gray-blue. Sima understood that such a dusky color meant a problem with blood flow, with a patient's heart. She'd asked Chief Resident Danielson about dark lips and cool hands and feet on patients when she made rounds with him and the interns.

Mr. Shtrom grunted again. He pursed his lips. Sima could hear his breathing, in and out, struggling to move air. He yanked his arm from her hold and the IV machine bleeped. She reached for the arm to save the IV from being pulled out, but his hand flailed toward her face. She ducked to avoid getting smacked. The old man coughed. His big hairy white hands gripped the side rails again.

"Go find the good doctor. She's in the on-call room," Miss Armstrong said.

THE ON-CALL ROOM SMELLED THE same as always, like dirty socks and running shoes. Sima found Dr. Kahn in fetal position on the bottom bunk. Working so many nights together that year, Sima watched her every move, trying to understand what it was like to be an intern. What it was like to be *this* insecure intern who struggled to get through each day and night. Dr. Kahn was just recently back from a week's mourning leave after her father's death. She rolled onto her back and stared at the rusty springs above her. Sima sat down on the edge of the bed.

"There's a new patient for you in the CCU. Miss Armstrong wants you to know," she said.

"I saw him in the ER," Mindy said and turned to the wall, her back to Sima.

Sima nudged her on the top of her head. "Nurse Armstrong needs you."

Somewhere between lunch in the Red Hat diner across the street from the hospital and the day they'd found Mindy's father dead, she had decided that Dr. Kahn had become her mentor. She didn't know exactly when this had happened but she admitted it now to herself: she wanted *to be* Mindy. And Mindy had invited Sima to call her by her first name.

Mindy's pager rested on the floor by the bed. It beeped but she didn't answer it. It beeped again. Why Chief Danielson didn't see that Mindy wasn't ready to be back taking care of cardiac patients Sima couldn't understand. Mindy's father had died of a heart attack.

Sima read the numbers flashing on the pager as it beeped

again. She shook Mindy's shoulders with both hands. "Miss Armstrong needs you."

Sima wanted urgently to be needed right now. She got an A in biology, in all her courses. Still, she'd put off taking English composition another semester once again.

Mindy moved closer to the wall behind the bed, pulled her knees tight into her chest.

The numbers on the pager flashed a second time. Sima turned to leave the on-call room.

IN THE CCU, MR. SHTROM STILL held tight to the bed rails. His hospital gown hung off his shoulders. He started to rock in the bed.

"Now, now," Miss Armstrong clicked her tongue. "All this fuss will get you nowhere."

"Where's Dr. Kahn?" she asked. "His heart rate is racing." Miss Armstrong looked up at the monitor as it bleeped rapidly above her patient's bed. "He signed out against medical advice from some tiny hospital in New Jersey. Bad heart attack. I need the doctor."

"She's coming." Sima could only hope this was true. She tried to straighten the hospital gown on the old man's shoulders.

Mr. Shtrom rustled the arm with the IV again and the

IV machine chirped. He pursed his lips harder. Suddenly his face got blue, then bluer.

"Get the bottle of nitro," Miss Armstrong shouted. "Top shelf on the desk."

The telephone was on the main desk in the CCU close to the door. Sima grabbed the phone and dialed the number to the on- call room. *Ring, ring.* Pick up the phone. She didn't want to imagine Mindy still lying there on her side, face to the wall.

"Hurry up with the damn nitro," Miss Armstrong's voice was louder. *"Then* page Kahn."

Sima dropped the phone and ran to the bed with the bottle of nitroglycerin pills.

"Under the tongue," Miss Armstrong said to Mr. Shtrom, her words firm but gentle.

Sima took a tiny pill between her thumb and forefinger. She didn't know the Ukrainian word for tongue so she tried the Polish one.

"Jezor," she said.

She lifted her hand to her own tongue and tapped it with her forefinger, and as she leaned in, the Star of David fell out of her scrub shirt right in front of Mr. Shtrom. His breathing got faster, shallower. He grabbed at his chest and shook his head side to side.

He shoved Sima's hand away. He grabbed the bed rails again. *"Nah, Juden, nah!"*

She listened to his breathing, more labored as his eyes bulged at the Star of David dangling between them. David. Davey. Her brother, her father's. At that moment, she wanted him to know who she was. And that she held the pill that could ease his pain.

She didn't hide the star. What kind of doctor would do that?

Then he hit his chest with both hands. His nostrils puffed out. *"Nah, nah."*

Mindy shuffled in through the door. And the next second, Mr. Shtrom was down. He fell back onto the pillow. His arms limp, his mouth wide open. Mindy stood there by the bed, not moving. She just stood there so still Sima could barely stand it. Was Mindy going to do something, call someone, breathe, talk, anything? For a moment, she didn't care.

"Page the code team," Mindy finally ordered. "Now!" And then Sima ran to the phone.

Mindy shoved down the side rails of the bed and got up on the mattress. Her knees were along one side of Mr. Shtrom's chest. She leaned over him, the heels of her hands balanced on his bare torso, and she started to pump on his heart. "Get him breathing," she said to Miss Armstrong.

Miss Armstrong placed the mouthpiece of the Ambu bag over the patient's blue lips. Sima watched Mr. Shtrom's chest move in and out, in and out. The overhead announced the code, and then came the *squeak, squeak* of running shoes into the room. The on-call doctors from all the medical wards in the hospital stampeded through the door into the CCU and surrounded the patient's bed.

The senior resident stood center stage. He looked up at the EKG monitor above the heads of everyone in the room. "Check the IV line," he called out.

One intern fingered the IV site, another one turned up the flow on the tubing.

"Push an amp of epi," the senior ordered. Miss Armstrong handed a syringe to the intern by the IV site. "Epi's in."

"Keep pumping," the senior ordered.

Mindy was still up on the side of the bed, on her knees alongside Mr. Shtrom. No one from the code team had taken over for her. Her forehead was wet with sweat and wrinkled with concentration. She leaned her hands onto the man's chest again and again as if *her* life depended on every compression.

One hand over the other, Sima pushed down on the air as if she were pumping in place of Mindy. Would she have taken over, given Mindy a break, if the room hadn't been filled with interns? She'd witnessed almost as many codes as they had. For a moment, she was satisfied there was no role for an orderly in this drama, other than to deliver a sample to the stat lab, or to go find a box of gauze pads.

"Where's anesthesia? We need to tube him," the senior shouted. "We can't wait. Miss Armstrong, an ET tube, a large one." He had Mr. Shtrom's head in his hands, extending his chin up and his neck back to the correct angle for inserting the endotracheal tube.

Sima stood at the far end of the bed now, away from the action of the code team. Her feet were covered with the torn paper wrappings of discarded 4 x 4 gauze pads, used alcohol swabs. The white bedsheets were specked with blood. Mr. Shtrom's feet stuck out of the sheets.

Then the senior resident suddenly called out, "Everyone, stand back." Mindy stopped pumping and got off the bed. The senior held up the paddles and then gave Mr. Shtrom a shock. The old man's body flailed for a second. "Resume pumping." And Mindy was back at her station.

"Does he have a pulse?" the senior asked. Mindy shook her head no.

"Stand back." He gave the patient a second shock, and a third.

"Everyone stop," he ordered, Mindy still pumping. He said it again, "Everyone stop."

Mindy, Miss Armstrong, the other interns, and Sima stood still so the team could assess the patient's response. Everyone watched the EKG monitor above the bed.

Flatline.

"Dr. Kahn?" the senior said.

Mindy looked at the clock on the wall by the door. "Time of death: 5:45 a.m."

AT 7:00 A.M., SIMA FOUND Mindy on the bottom of the bunk bed in the on-call room, Mr. Shtrom's chart open in her lap. Her white jacket was in a ball on the pillow. She was still in scrubs. She hadn't taken a shower yet.

"The nurses need the chart," Sima said.

Mindy didn't look up. "I have to write the death note," she said blankly.

"They're getting him ready for the morgue," Sima said. "They paged me to take him down." Trips to the morgue were the worst part of being an orderly, even when she didn't know the patient. But this patient, this Ukrainian patient. She had held the tiny nitroglycerin pill and she'd let him push it away. She tried to imagine if she'd been his doctor.

The door to the on-call room opened. Chief Resident Danielson stepped in. He sat down quietly on the other side of Mindy. He wasn't known to come into the hospital this early, and he rarely made appearances in the on-call room. Sima didn't think his presence, quiet as it seemed to be that moment, was a good sign.

"Sima, I need to speak with Dr. Kahn," he said.

Sima paused in the hall at the partly opened door. She heard Chief Danielson ask for the chart. She heard him flipping pages.

"He was in big trouble the minute he walked in the door," he said.

Silence. Then she heard Mindy say, in monotone, "I should have done another EKG."

"This guy was a goner before he got here," Chief Danielson stated as if it were fact. "But yes, you should have done another EKG. It wouldn't have made any difference, but that's what you should have done when Miss Armstrong paged you."

Sima was grateful Chief Danielson invited her on rounds with the interns, but she could tell he liked to see them squirm when he asked questions. She wasn't sure she wanted to be an intern on his watch. He should have known Mindy wouldn't do well in the CCU so soon. He could have assigned her to a regular medical ward. Or Neuro. Nothing big ever happened on Neuro. He had taught Sima a lot, he'd offered to write her a letter of recommendation. What would he think if he'd seen her with Mr. Shtrom?

She put her head into the room. "The nurses need the chart," she said.

Chief Danielson put his hands into the pockets of his long chief resident coat. "Please write the note and notify the family, Dr. Kahn."

"They probably don't speak English," Sima said.

"Dr. Kahn can handle it," Chief Danielson said.

Sima didn't understand how he could be so sure.

Chief Danielson didn't make eye contact with either of them. He straightened his coat and stepped out.

MINDY STARED DOWN AT THE pink progress note pages, her hands glued to the blue plastic chart. She sat motionless, like a statue of herself.

Sima waited by the door.

Mindy spoke. "Patient died. The end."

"That's not what you're supposed to write," Sima said. "You answered the page, you were there when I wasn't. *You* write the note."

Mindy's pen slid off the chart onto the floor. She kicked it across the room and it disappeared under the opposite bunk. The chart slipped off her lap onto the floor.

Sima picked up the pen. "Maybe the senior could write the note." She sat down next to Mindy, both of them now crosslegged on the floor. She picked up the chart and held it out to her. When Mindy made no eye contact, Sima lowered the chart onto her own lap. She opened it to the next clean page. And then she began to write. She read out loud what she wrote.

"Death note: Called to see patient having chest pain at 5:15 a.m. He was in cardiac arrest."

Mindy closed her eyes and didn't say anything. Sima continued to write and read.

"The code team was called. Three rounds of cardiac medications were given and three shocks with no response. The patient had signed out AMA from another hospital the second day after a massive anterior wall MI. The patient was pronounced dead at 5:45 a.m. Family will be notified."

Sima placed the chart in Mindy's lap. Mindy opened her eyes and stared at the note.

"Nothing here is inaccurate," Sima said and handed Mindy her pen.

THE SHTROM FAMILY HUDDLED IN the corridor outside the double doors to the CCU: a clan of people pacing and mumbling to each other, short and not-so-short, skinny and round, some with curly brown hair and some blond, two or three wearing glasses and hats, the babushkas clutching purses to their chests. That was all Sima could see at first of these of Old Country people Aunt Miriam left Poland to get away from. They sounded like an unruly school brood at recess. When she was little, the children of these people threw rotten tomatoes at her, spit at her. *Kike,* dirty Jew. She didn't pull out her Star of David and wave it in their faces. But at that very moment she wanted them to feel what she had seen in her own father's eyes when a Ukrainian doctor said he couldn't do anything for the son of a Jew, and her baby brother died and her father was never the same again. Her mother couldn't forgive her father. And Sima's life was never the same again.

A woman in an ankle-length brown dress set a large bowl of potatoes and onions covered in plastic down on the floor. Immigrant families often brought bowls of food that smelled of home. She elbowed the man standing next to a very old woman.

"*Trymayte yiyi*," she said. Hold onto her.

"I'm Dr. Kahn," Mindy said. "Does anyone in the family speak English?"

A little blond boy with a cowlick squirmed up close to Mindy. He reached into Mindy's jacket pocket. One of the babushkas grabbed him by the arm and yanked him away.

Mindy folded her arms across her chest. "We need a translator," she said.

"Sima here speaks their language," Miss Armstrong said to Mindy.

"You're Polish," Mindy said.

"Ukrainian and Polish are similar," Sima replied.

She couldn't look at Mindy. She couldn't bear to look at Mrs. Shtrom or the rest of the family. "The words are a little different, but we can understand each other."

Miss Armstrong lead the family to the Isolation Room, where they moved patients with contagious diseases, the only area with any privacy. There was a single bed with an un-sheeted mattress, no pillow, and one chair at the far end away from the door.

One family member huddled to the next.

Sima scanned the clan. The room felt like a coffin.

Mindy stationed herself against one wall. Her hands gripped the ends of the stethoscope hanging around her neck. "Tell Mrs. Shtrom her husband had a very bad heart."

Sima's first words came out too loud. *"Twoj maz mail slabe serce,"* she said in Polish. Your husband had a bad heart. She wasn't a doctor but she knew: first do no harm.

When Sima stopped talking, Mrs. Shtrom's mouth wrinkled into a hole.

"Bad heart?" the woman in the long brown dress said, in broken English. Sima noticed the embroidery down one sleeve of the dress. Red and green with tiny threads of blue, hand sewn. Their eyes met for a long moment. Sima nodded to confirm.

The daughter squeezed her mother's arm. She put her free hand up to her chest and struck it. "Bad heart," the daughter said. *"Yah."*

"Tell her he had a heart attack at the other hospital," Mindy said.

Miss Armstrong pulled the chair out from the wall. "Let Mrs. Shtrom sit down," she said.

"*Twoja matka powinna usiasc,*" Sima said in Polish to the daughter. Your mother should sit down.

The sleeve of the daughter's dress brushed up alongside Sima's bare, weary arm. She leaned into the softness for a moment, caught the eye of the daughter. Then she moved closer to one side of Mrs. Shtrom, closer to the smell of boiled onion, and helped the daughter settle her mother the way she and Miss Armstrong had not been able to do with the old man in the CCU.

Mindy bumped into the unmade bed and the bed knocked against the wall. The sound of creaky metal wheels on hospital tile jolted everyone in the room.

The daughter leaned in toward Sima. "*Moze sz mi powiediec o mojm ojou,*" she said. Tell me, please, about my father. Sima felt her own heart beat quicken. Her own father, she could see his face. And then the cowlick boy stepped out. He grabbed hold of the finger of the rubber glove sticking from Mindy's pocket and pulled on it. *Snap, snap, snap.*

Mindy stood there, a sullen face on. "He should have stayed at the hospital in New Jersey," she said. "Why didn't he stay there?"

Miss Armstrong glared at Mindy. "Dr. Kahn," was all she said.

Sima yanked the glove out of Mindy's pocket and handed it to the boy. *"Serce Waszego ojca był zły przy innym szpital,"* she said to the daughter. Your father's heart was bad at the other hospital. First do no harm.

The child held the glove up to Mindy.

Mrs. Shtrom and her daughter talked back and forth to each other. *"Zły szpital,"* Mrs. Shtrom said. Bad hospital. Bad hospital. The daughter looked at Sima. *"My balismy sie tam. Nikt mówił nasz język,"* she said. We were afraid there. No one spoke our language. "No stay." First do no harm.

Polish words came out of Sima's mouth, and Ukrainian words came back at her. *Papa* this and *Papa* that, *Papa* the same in any language. Back and forth, the foreign words filled the air, Polish, Ukrainian, broken English.

"They want to see Mr. Shtrom," Sima said. And then she wanted to tell the daughter that Mindy had just lost her father too. It was a doctor's job to attend to strangers, to put aside the pain of dead fathers and persecution for the moment and yet connect with it all at the same time.

"That's all they said?" Mindy sank back into the bed.

The boy put the glove up to his mouth and blew.

Sima surveyed the room—Mindy, the motley troupe of family members standing quietly now, the old woman, the daughter. The boy breathing hard the only sound in the room.

She knelt beside the daughter on the floor by Mrs. Shtrom. They were two young women without fathers. Her own *Papa* lost to six-year-old Sima long before he died. Something in Sima let the Old Country fall away. She looked up at Mindy, then back to the daughter. They were three. Not Ukrainian, not Polish, not American.

"Ja też stracił mojego ojca," Sima said to the daughter. I too have lost my father. *"Doktor po prostu stracił jej ojca. Rozumiemy."* The doctor just lost her father. We understand.

The boy continued blowing into the glove, the fingers stretching bigger and longer. Everyone in the room watched the boy's cheek puff out as he blew. He took another breath, and then he lost his grip. The air inside the glove farted back into his face and the glove shot out of his hands. It shriveled to the floor. The boy laughed with his whole body.

"We gave him medication for his chest pain," Mindy blurted out over the laughter.

The daughter reached for Mindy. "Die?" she said. "Papa die?"

Mindy nodded, her face a blank.

The old woman raised her eyes to Sima, who was kneeling still alongside her daughter. She put a hand to Sima's face.

Sima took the old woman's hand and held it between her two hands. She nodded. *"Twoj maz nie zyje,"* she said.

Your husband has died. She nodded to the daughter. Your father is dead.

Mrs. Shtrom's head tilted back, her eyes closed. She leaned into her daughter who was standing by the side of the chair.

"Ne Pravda!" This can't be. The old woman rocked back and forth in her seat. The chair shifted off center, threatening to tip.

"Mama," the daughter said. She put her arms around her mother, both of them wailing. Then the little boy began to cry. The daughter reached for the hand of the boy. She pulled him toward the chair, enclosed him in with her mother. The little boy's cries were muffled in the clothes of his elders. The other family members stepped in closer.

Miss Armstrong leaned toward the old woman. She smoothed the sweater bunched at the widow's shoulders. "Let's get her onto the bed," she said to Sima.

Over her shoulder, Sima saw Mindy leaning back against the bed, her face pale, the face of her mentor, her friend. She glanced at the family, the daughter holding her mother and the boy, and up at Miss Armstrong.

"We can handle this," Sima said.

"Yes," Miss Armstrong said. "I believe you can."

13

No Mangoes for Mindy

Sima saw Mindy emptying her pockets onto the counter at the laundry, handing in her dirty white jacket. Mindy turned and walked away. Sima was close enough to hear the laundry lady shout, "Hey, you forgot your clean jacket!"

Sima stepped up to the counter. "I'll give it to her."

She clutched the clean white intern cloak, still warm from the laundry, and trotted down the tunnel hallway past the mummy pipes. The meeting with the Shtrom family had been two days before and she hadn't seen Mindy since.

She tapped her on the shoulder. "You forgot your jacket."

A brown paper bag in one hand, her head down, Mindy walked on.

"They were looking for you to sign the death certificate on Mr. Shtrom yesterday," Sima found herself shouting to Mindy's back.

"I signed it." Her words were measured, careful, calm. She kept moving down the tunnel.

Sima could barely keep pace. "Could you slow up a minute?"

Mindy stopped at the elevator to A-building. She clutched her bag to her chest.

"What's in the bag?" Sima reached her arm out. "Here's your clean jacket."

Mindy turned away. "You're the big hero now," she said.

"What are you talking about?"

Mindy's wire rims were crooked, her hair disheveled as if she was post-call.

"Sima, the translator."

"All I did was talk to a few Ukrainians," Sima said.

"But you didn't put your arms around that old lady until Miss Armstrong made you pick her up off the floor."

"I was doing my job," Sima said. "What's going on?"

"It's none of your business." Mindy punched the UP button on the elevator.

"Why is it none of my business?"

"The way I walk, the way I talk, my hair. It's always your business. Why can't you just leave me alone?"

"I thought we were friends," Sima said. She held out the jacket like a white flag.

"Friends don't make each other look bad."

The elevator door opened.

"You better get up to the ward," Mindy said. "They're waiting for those labs you got." Sima stepped in, Mindy didn't follow her. The doors closed.

A FRUIT BASKET SAT ON the counter at the A71 Nurses' Station: mangoes and papayas and plantains, all shades of yellow. Island fruits like so many of the nurses and aides ate for lunch every day. It was the first time Sima had seen a fruit basket delivered to the wards. She had never touched a mango. The skin was smooth.

"Them mangoes is not for you, Sima." Miss Parker, the ward clerk, slapped Sima's hand. She stood straight in her brown polyester skirt suit, ID dangling from a silver beaded chain around her neck. She put her arms around the basket as if it were alive, scooped it to her chest, and walked into the Doctors' Charting Room. Sima followed with the labs slips.

Steinberg, future ophthalmologist, his tortoiseshell horn rims halfway down his nose, was buried in a chart. He rocked into his text as if he were studying a passage from the Talmud. Dr. Long, ex-surgical intern, had his feet up on a chair with an open chart in his lap.

Miss Parker marched in and placed the fruit basket in the middle of the counter. She slapped Dr. Long's leg. "Maybe you sit that way in your house," she said, "but not in mine."

Dr. Long stood up and returned his chart to the rack. "I didn't know you could walk, Miss Parker."

"This here fruit is from Mrs. Sampson, the lady with breast cancer," she said. "It's for Dr. Kahn, but since she won't be around for a while, I'm sure Mrs. Sampson don't want it to go to waste. All you doctors take care of her when you's on-call anyway."

Miss Armstrong brushed by Sima with an armful of charts. She elbowed the fruit basket to dump them next to Steinberg. Chief Danielson stepped in behind her.

"Rounds in ten minutes. We'll reassign Dr. Kahn's patients." The chief nodded at Steinberg and Dr. Long.

Miss Armstrong rested a hand on Sima's shoulder. "You did good with the Shtrom family," she said. "You could make a career for yourself translating. They pay people to do that in some hospitals." She turned to leave, then added, "Chief Danielson wants to talk with you before rounds."

Everyone left the room.

Chief Danielson sat down at the counter. He pulled a large envelope from under his arms and spread the contents out before them. He flipped through pages of pink progress notes, then landed on the last entry: *Death note*. "What do you think of this?"

Sima kept a small spiral notebook when she was invited on rounds with the medical students. The Chief told her to take notes and later asked her what she had learned. He had never reviewed a chart with her. She sat down and stared at the page. She had no idea what he wanted to know.

"Please read it," he said.

Sima didn't need to read the note but she took a few minutes to scan the words, now a blur. *Nothing is inaccurate.* But she wasn't a doctor, she had no authority to know.

"Were you there when Mr. Shtrom coded?"

"Yes," she said. Miss Armstrong saw her hold the nitroglycerin pill under the man's tongue. What else had she told Chief Danielson?"

"Do you know who is responsible for this note?"

"Dr. Kahn," she said. That was not inaccurate. She wasn't going to say anymore.

Chief Danielson collected the loose pages of the chart back into the large envelope. "There's going to be a case review," he said and headed for the door. "You'll be expected to attend."

14

Visiting Hours

Visiting hours were over and Mrs. Sampson needed another X-ray. It should have been Mindy's order, her night on-call, but Chief Danielson had decided she needed more time to get over the death of her father: Mindy was on a leave of absence. Sima worried Mindy had messed up so badly with Mr. Shtrom and the family that she might not be allowed to return. Talking with the family, Sima was doing something no one else in the room could do. She'd stepped up, Miss Armstrong said. She'd make a good trans-lator, Miss Armstrong said. Maybe she should listen to her mama and just aim for "a more better job." Maybe the Chief knew more, maybe he was disappointed in her too, and she wouldn't be invited on rounds anymore.

Outside the six-bedded Female Room, Sima heard voices. A figure in black stood by Mrs. Sampson's bed. Her hair was matted as if she'd worked a double shift wearing a hairnet instead of a hat, which would have made more sense now in December in New York City. She wore a long black coat and, peeking out from the sleeves, Sima could see her bony wrists. Out the bottom of the coat where it was unbuttoned were stick-straight legs devoid of any muscle, almost as skinny as her wrists and covered in fishnet stockings below a miniskirt.

The woman tapped her foot on the floor, and then walked to the night table by the bedside where Mrs. Sampson's cloth bag of sewing things rested. She bumped her thigh into the bed, which jostled it a bit.

"So where is it?" the woman said to Mrs. Sampson.

"Mrs. Sampson," Sima said, "they want you downstairs for an X-ray."

The woman didn't look up. Suddenly she was focused on the sleeve of her heavy coat. She picked at a white spot, scratched at it. She reached into the sleeve and pulled out a tissue. She scrunched her nose, then sniffed, and blew into the tissue, then stuffed the ratty material back into her sleeve.

"She ain't going nowhere till she tells me where it is," the woman muttered.

"Visiting hours are over," Sima said. She moved the wheelchair to the side of the bed closest to the door; the woman stood on the other side, her arms crossed over her chest now.

"We ain't having no visit," Mrs. Sampson said.

Mrs. Sampson's face was drawn, long. Her eyes were half closed. Sima stared at those eyes, as if looking at them would make them open fully so she could get a hint at what the old woman was feeling about this no-visit visitor.

The woman in black sniffed again. "Ain't got all day," she said. Her words were defiant but her tone was sad. She kept her head down, her chin almost onto her chest. She stood there like a petulant child, refusing to engage, the way Sima often stood against *her* mother.

Sima said to the woman, "You'll have to leave now."

Mrs. Sampson raised her arm and swatted the air in the direction of the woman. "Go back to your own world," she said. She picked up Sammy's shirt from her lap and began to fold it.

"You still sewing," the woman said. "You was always sewing." She reached over the bed toward the button edge of the shirt. "You never sewed for me like that."

"I sewed for you plenty when you were his age." Mrs. Sampson pulled the shirt in closer. She smoothed out wrinkles with her hands and folded the shirt a second time.

Sima thought she saw Mrs. Sampson begin to look up at the sorry woman standing by her bedside but then Mrs. Sampson's head bent over further, her chin into her chest the way the woman's had been.

The woman reached toward the shirt again, and this time she grabbed it from Mrs. Sampson. She held the small shirt out in front of her, touched the buttons, the collar. Then she put it up to her face, rubbed the cloth against her cheek. "I can smell him, my boy."

"It's too clean for you to smell anything." Mrs. Sampson's eyes widened. She leaned forward to retrieve the shirt but the woman stepped back from Mrs. Sampson's reach. "You never put a clean shirt on him."

"I had to take care of myself. Wasn't no one else to do it."

"You wouldn't let anyone take care of you."

Sima's own mother accused her of the very same thing. Suddenly she was back in the dining room of their apartment at the open drawer of the china cabinet, her mother's hand landing on top of Sima's with a hard slap.

"Why don't you show her Sammy's photograph?" Sima said to Mrs. Sampson.

"You got a picture of him? Give it to me—you owe me that much."

"I don't owe you nothing when it comes to Sammy."

"He's my son, not yours. My flesh and blood. You didn't birth him."

Mrs. Sampson slid the photograph out of the pocket of her robe. It was sealed in clear plastic.

The daughter stepped around the bed, close to her mother. She reached out one finger to the clear cover. "I've touched him now," she said softly. The sides of her mouth turned down as though she were about to cry.

"That photograph is to make *me* feel close," Mrs. Sampson said. She pulled the photograph into her chest. "You gave away your right to feel that."

"He's mine," the daughter said.

"I can't live without him." Mrs. Sampson looked as though she were about to cry, and she reached away with the photograph for Sima to take hold of it.

"Give it here," the daughter said.

Sima wanted the daughter to see the photograph, the way she wanted to see the photograph of her baby brother. She took it directly from Mrs. Sampson.

"He's not yours," the daughter said.

"I'm going to adopt him. Make him mine."

Sima stared at Mrs. Sampson, at the daughter. She knew how much she wanted, needed, begged for her own mother to love her. How much it hurt to love her back, how hard it was.

"Nobody's going to let an old dying woman adopt a child when his mother is right here."

"So that's why you're here." Mrs. Sampson got red in the face. "You want to steal him from me in my last days. And I thought maybe you wanted to see your mother one more time before it was too late."

The daughter had her grubby fingers on the edge of the photograph now. Sima tried to hold onto it, but the plastic was slick. And then the photograph slipped from her hand and into the daughter's. The eyes of the three women were locked on the photograph for what seemed like a long time. If only the mother and daughter could bear to look at each other, could see all the pain. And the love.

"Your sister can adopt him. She takes care of him when I'm in here."

"That bitch," she huffed. "You've always loved her best."

Then the daughter moved to the other side of the bed. She dropped Sammy's shirt on Mrs. Sampson's lap. She held onto the photograph. She pulled Mrs. Sampson's purse from the drawer of the night table. She turned the purse upside down, dumped the contents onto the bed.

She put the photograph into the bosom of her coat and picked up a bottle. "Morphine sulfate," she read. She unscrewed the lid and took out two pills. She put one in her mouth and swallowed it. She held the second pill under her mother's nose. "This is what we have in common now, old lady."

Mrs. Sampson turned her face away from the pill but the daughter's hand followed and the pill was there again, in front of her. Mrs. Sampson closed her eyes. She shook her head.

Sima could see Mrs. Sampson's breath growing fast, she could hear it getting wheezy. She pushed the daughter's hand away from her mother's face. "Take the pills and get out."

The daughter sneered at Sima. "Big shot. You the one who give me the photograph."

"Leave now. Or I'll call security."

The daughter held tight to the bottle of pills. She put her other hand up to her chest. "I got the photograph."

Mrs. Sampson kept her eyes closed. "Keep it," she said.

The daughter backed away from the bed and slinked around the corner, out the door.

Sima sat down on the edge of the bed next to Mrs. Sampson. She fingered the buttons on Sammy's shirt where it lay between them. "I'm sorry about the picture," she said.

Mrs. Sampson opened her eyes. "Don't make no never mind. That's all she got left."

15

Family Photos

Sima saw her mama step into the elevator of their building as the doors closed. She took the stairs, two steps at a time, up all four flights.

Her mother had left a small grocery bag by the front door of their apartment, the door opened. Sima carried the bag inside, set it down, and turned the inside bolt to lock the door.

She dropped her backpack by the door, didn't bother to take off her coat and hat. She headed directly to the dining room cabinet.

She pulled open the narrow drawer on the left side. She lifted the envelopes, large and small, and emptied them onto the dining room table. And then her mother's shadow was over her shoulder, her mother still in her winter coat standing by her side. Two curly haired heads staring at a pile of black-and-whites, three-by-fives. Neither of them said a word. Sima could feel the cold air between them.

Sima lifted one photograph. Her mother and father standing close together, she at one end holding onto her mother's gloved hand, her father holding a baby.

"Tell me about him," Sima said in Polish.

Her mother stood silently.

Sima waved the photograph in front of her mother's face.

"This boy, this baby."

"That boy, that baby boy," her mother said. "He was not my first boy. I lost the first one before this one was born, in a bucket, in the bathroom. His little boy parts, those tiny toes. *He* was supposed to be David."

Her mother's words rushed out of her, as if she couldn't wait to be free of them. The expression on her mother's face was sadder than sad. There was a heaviness in her eyes, in the drooping skin alongside her mouth, that Sima had never seen before. She was almost sorry she had pulled out the photographs. She had betrayed her mother the way she had almost betrayed Mrs. Sampson.

Her mother picked up a photograph of people holding drinks, candlelight in the background, so happy, happy, eating and smiling, happy.

"This was his bris," her mother said. "You had to hold down his legs while Lesk did his circumcision. All I did was cry. Cry."

In that tiny, dark room in the basement of the building

in Poland, holding tight to the little pink legs of her baby brother. Why was *she* the one who had to hold the baby's legs still? Was she the only child there other than her baby brother? It was stuffy and crowded. Every Jew in the village was packed into that small, windowless room.

"We were like sardines down there," her mother said.

Sima remembered her mother crying, wailing more loudly than her brother.

"Why were you crying, Mama?" Sima said.

"I didn't want for him to be circumcised. I feared for his life, for when he went to school and the other boys would know. I didn't want that for him," she said. "But your father, he insisted." And now her mother was crying beside her.

And then Sima remembered the night the doctor came to visit. It was not many days after the circumcision and the baby wouldn't sleep. He was crying and screaming. Her mother was up walking the floor with him, her father was yelling at her to go back to sleep, that the baby would be fine in the morning.

"Why did he die, Mama?" Sima said.

"Your brother had a fever," her mother said. "His little face was all red from crying. His little penis was swollen. I insisted your father get a doctor. And then a doctor came." Her mother stopped talking. She fingered the photograph of the party, of the baby in a blanket in her arms in another picture. She reached for the one covered in tissue paper but didn't open it.

"The doctor was Ukrainian," she said. "He understood perfectly our Polish, his Polish. We were all Polish."

Her mother grew very quiet, her breath slow. The hand reaching for the yellowed black-and-white photograph was shaking.

"The doctor saw the baby's penis with the skin cut off. He dropped the sheet on his body. *'Juden,'* he snickered. He would do nothing. He ran out the door."

"Did Papa find another doctor?" Sima asked.

"The next morning, my David was blue. My baby was blue. He had turned on himself, crying so hard, and he wasn't breathing." Her mother sat silently in the chair. Her head down, her eyes on the photograph of the baby in her arms.

"Why didn't Papa get another doctor?" Sima said.

"'No Ukrainian doctors,' your father said. 'No more doctors.'"

"Why didn't you insist, Mama?" Sima said.

"Why? Why?" her mother said. "Ask your dead Papa why. He wanted you should become doctor. How was that going to save my David?"

"Papa said I should become a doctor?" Sima stared at her mother.

"Doctors deal with death, and dead people," her mother said. She reached for the photograph but Sima's hand landed on it first.

"Doctors do more than that," Sima said. "I *could* become a doctor." She could.

"A more better job," her mother said. "It's enough."

Her mother slapped her hand hard. "My son." She hit Sima's hand with both hands now.

Sima grabbed her mother's hands with her free one and pried them off.

Her mother's arms flailed in the air between them. "Enough is enough." And then she slapped Sima on the face.

Sima stood silent, stunned by the sting. She held back the urge to slap her mother back. She could see now how her mother denied her, had denied her father, and her brother. Her mother, a head shorter, still strong and as willful as she'd ever been. The will that allowed her to sell her husband's heirlooms after he died and bring her daughter so far away to a new place.

"Is it enough Mama?" Sima said. "Is it really?"

16

Four H

The ward was dark as usual the next night except for lights that glowed low along the hallway wall outside the six-patient rooms. It was past midnight and Sima would be up all night, same as the doctors on call, though they had rooms to sleep in when they finished their work, mostly free of cockroaches, and air conditioned. Sima put her feet up on the footrest of a geri chair in the hall by the Nurses' Station, pulled a blanket up to her chin. She'd barely closed her eyes when voices boomed and bounced off the walls in invisible currents.

"He won't budge," a big male voice said.

"What do you mean, he won't budge?" a second big voice said. "Tell him to get his butt out of there."

"You do it," the first voice said.

"I ain't going to do it."

Sima put her fingers in her ears and then she felt a nudge on her shoulder.

"You've got to come." Nurse Bailey's Jamaican twang rang true.

"Why?" Sima pulled the blanket in closer. "You should page the intern."

"Just come." Nurse Bailey's voice trailed off. She wasn't one to insist for no reason. Sima pushed down on the footrest and left the blanket on the chair.

Around the corner, two hospital police, big guys in blue, stood across from the elevator. One cop wore a cap and the other had a billy club hanging off his belt. It looked like Mr. Biggs, the elevator man, had gone off on break and left the elevator door open. Inside the metal box stood Skinny in his hospital gown. His arms hung so long they nearly reached his bony knees.

"What's going on?" Sima asked.

The cop wearing the cap smirked. "She wants to know what's going on."

Nurse Bailey elbowed Sima. She pointed to the elevator. "Skinny's been in there for forty-five minutes now."

"Just standing there?" Sima said.

"He's taken the elevator hostage," the cop huffed.

"Come on, guys." Sima chuckled.

"You can see for yourself, missy," one cop said. "This here patient won't budge."

Skinny was taller by a head than either of these men in blue, but the cops' wrists were bigger around than Skinny's thigh. Skinny wasn't threatening either of them, or Nurse Bailey. He was just staring into the air in front of him, out the elevator door.

"Etienne?" Sima called, using his Haitian name. Etienne, like Sima's mother, didn't speak a word of English. She stepped toward the elevator, and tried a few words in French. Not Haitian French but the Parisian French she'd learned in seventh grade. *"Venez ici."* Come here. Skinny would understand this kind of French better than the Ukrainians understood her Polish.

Skinny glanced at Sima, and then lowered himself into Mr. Biggs's elevator chair.

The second cop yanked the billy club from his belt. He hit the palm of his hand with it and swung it in the air.

"This isn't a Western shootout," Sima said. "Just get Skinny off the elevator. He's a toothpick—you guys can handle him." Sima's French wasn't good enough to ask Skinny what he was doing there. She figured he wanted to go for a walk but got confused or scared. With the second set of elevators not working, his presence there was clearly a problem.

"You get him off," the cop wearing the cap said to Sima.

"He's a foot taller than me," Sima said. "You do it. He doesn't bite."

"Maybe he does. Who knows? Not going to let one of *those* kind touch me."

The *Times* had reports about parents afraid to drink out of the cup of a gay son with the new disease or even eat at the same table, but Sima had never seen County hospital police behave this way. The new disease was called GRID, Gay-Related Immunodeficiency Syndrome, and struck sick the four Hs: homosexuals, heroin addicts, hemophiliacs, and Haitians—like Skinny. All anyone knew for sure was that it had to do with blood. And at the County, where the house officers—the interns—had to do their own blood draws, hospital chiefs worried there would soon be a fifth kind of H getting deathly ill. Not hospital cops.

The elevator door closed and Skinny disappeared.

Sima, Nurse Bailey, and the two cops stared at the closed doors. Nobody said a word. They stood around for what seemed like a long time to Sima, who just wanted to get back to the geri chair. The cops paced the floor and muttered about calling for more security. Nurse Bailey pulled out her list of important telephone numbers to call in times like this. Then she started to head back to the ward to write up an incident report when they all heard the click of shoes coming down the hall. A ward clerk, not old wrinkly face Parker but a young woman in an African turban Sima had never seen before arrived on the scene.

"That patient, Etienne something or other, bed six, the tall one," she said.

They all turned in tandem—Sima, Nurse Bailey and the two cops.

"He's wandered downstairs to the ER, and somebody's got to bring him back." They watched silently as the ward clerk's head turned and the colorful shape of her turban angled over her torso back down the hallway.

Nurse Bailey said, "Sima, you go. Skinny likes you."

"It's always me."

"Go on." She nudged Sima's shoulder. "You speak French. You're a translator, a natural."

The second set of elevators out of order, Sima double-stepped the six flights down from A71 to the ER. The stairwell reeked of piss. The floor was sticky underfoot. Cigarette butts, empty Coke cans, a crumpled bus transfer glued to the wall. It was rumored a patient had once been found dead in this very stairwell.

The Male Room, the men's side of the ER, was wall-to-wall brown bodies half naked, sweating or shivering under piles of white blankets—no curtains pulled around any of them. Muscular arms and scarred ones held on to IV poles. Scruffy-haired heads leaned back into stiff pillows. Puffy eyes and swollen ankles, coughs and groans. The room was flooded with pain, fevers, fears, and foul words from foul mouths. Sima blocked out the smell of dirty socks and dirty bodies.

At the back of the room in a chair by the clerk's desk sat Skinny.

From the door, his eyes looked even deeper than they had in the elevator. His hollow cheeks sunken between bone. Like the faces in the newspaper cartoons of Jews in Poland.

Sima moved through the tangle of beds. "Etienne," she said. She knew more Ukrainian than French. "Are you all right?" she said in English.

Skinny just stared. Sitting in the chair, his head was almost to Sima's chin. His chest moved air in and out right before her. She could hear his silence. The way she'd heard her father's when he sat on the sofa and the wintery wind blew outside their house in Poland, around the edges of the living room.

IT WAS THE YEAR AFTER her brother died, one of the few moments when her parents didn't argue about selling the blue glass, her father's heirloom—all that was left of his family after the war—so they could move to America and Sima could have a future. It was all about Sima, her mother insisted; her father refused to talk about leaving Poland. "Over my dead body, over the dead body of my brother." Her mother spit at the air, "So be it." It was a quiet moment.

No shouting, no ranting. Her father sat on the sofa and her mother rubbed one of her father's hands, Sima held tight to the other. Her father leaned into her mother.

"Mama," her father said.

Her mother fingered his dark hair and pulled him closer. "It's OK, Papa."

"Go to the attic," her father said.

Then her father nosed a button of her mother's blouse, and started to whimper. Her mother closed her eyes, and then opened them.

"Sima, the attic," her mother said.

They didn't have an attic.

Sima climbed the stairs to her bedroom and sat by the window, watching branches blow in the wind, the way the snow sat on them an inch thick. Sometimes she had to sit there until it was dark outside. Her father needed her to go away and it was OK with her mother. These times she felt there was no one in the world she could count on. She worried that one day her mother wouldn't come upstairs to get her, and she wouldn't know what to do. She felt so alone. Invisible. As if an uncertain movement in the world might make her disappear into thin air.

SHE MOVED HER HAND TO Skinny's wrist, laid the other on his exposed knee.

"Come on, Etienne," Sima said. "Let's go back to the ward. *Venez avec moi.*"

She lifted Skinny's hand in her own, his brown-tan skin against the white-pink of hers. He felt soft and warm, just like anyone.

Skinny held Sima's hand against her knee, and stood, all six feet and more of him, their two hands dangling somewhere between his hospital johnny and her scrubs, and headed back to the ward.

Part Three

17

Finding the Pain

Mindy stood by the Nurses Station with a radiology request in hand. Chief Danielson had asked her to come back early from the leave *he'd* recommended because another intern had suddenly taken sick. Sima was pleased to see her mentor and friend still in the program. She hoped they were still friends. They hadn't spoken since the day by the laundry. She didn't have Mindy's telephone number, she didn't know where she lived.

"I paged you several times while you were gone," Sima said.

"My pager was turned off," Mindy said. She reached for a chart.

"Of course. You weren't working," Sima said. "I didn't think of that." She had but she didn't think anyone would tell her how to find Mindy. She wasn't sure she should even ask.

Mindy opened the chart, pried apart the page binders, and inserted the radiology request.

"I'm glad you're back."

"Mrs. Sampson needs a CT."

Business as usual.

THE PROBLEM THIS TIME WAS pain. Mrs. Sampson bit at her bottom lip. She stood from her perch on the side of the bed and slipped down into the wheelchair. She let her breath out, pursed her lips, and then closed her eyes.

"Sammy wants to know if I'm going to die out like the dinosaurs at the Natural History Museum. Six years old and he knows more than your doctors," she said to Sima.

Mindy stood bedside with the CT request, chart in hand. The X-ray tech had driven in from Staten Island on a Sunday night. He refused to do the CT unless Mindy's senior resident told him it was necessary.

Back pain in a cancer patient. There was no time to waste. If the pain was due to the spread of the breast cancer, it could be a few hours from pain to paralysis. It was one of those moments Sima had witnessed more and more during that year when Mindy lost her Boston cool and acted as if she'd grown up on the streets of New York City. Mindy had learned after so many months at the County that the only way to get urgent things done urgently was to be there with the patient. That's what it took. And Sima wanted again to be there, alongside her friend.

The three ladies left the ward on the long trek through the dank corridors of the tunnel to C-building where CT was. Wisps of baby-fine hair stuck out from beneath the blue bandana on Mrs. Sampson's head. Mindy's hair, like Sima's own, curled in the humidity of the wet steam from the mummy pipes, winter or summer.

Mrs. Sampson wheezed. "Hold up a minute," she said. "Hard to ride and rest at the same time."

Mindy tapped her watch. "They're waiting for us," she said. Sima elbowed her, and Mindy lowered her watch arm to her side.

The steam hissed from the mummy pipes, the water dripping from the rusted-out valves making orange stains on the floor. The air was heavy, hard to breathe in even if you were healthy, smelling of mold and damp concrete. Two flies bumped against the ceiling bulb, buzzing the way light-crazed bugs do.

Mrs. Sampson hitched up one hip, trying to find a more comfortable spot in her chair.

"Smells like my mother's cedar closet down here," Mindy said. "Her fur coat in mothballs. That's what she wanted—that and a diamond."

"Furs and diamonds don't make a woman happy," Mrs. Sampson said.

"I have a pearl," Sima said.

Mindy said, "A pearl—both my grandmothers gave me a string of them."

"Aunt Miriam gave me the pearl." Sima had never met either of her grandmothers; Mindy had two.

"It's the '80s," Mindy said. "Women join protests against killing animals for fur. And they want more than a fancy stone to pawn off to feed their fatherless kids."

Mrs. Sampson leaned into the wheelchair arm, hitched up off the other hip. "What's a girl like you know about fatherless kids?"

Mindy's arms dropped by her side. She faced the long hallway and walked off ahead.

"Her father just died," Sima said.

Mindy moved further away, her shoulders rolled in, head down.

Sima turned Mrs. Sampson's wheelchair and pushed it down the hallway. They slowed where Mindy stopped, leaning against the wall under a broken lightbulb. Mindy slumped down onto the floor, her back against a spot of dry wall where there were no mummy pipes.

Sima took a seat next to her, leg to leg, hip to hip, on the grimy, cold cement. She could feel Mindy trembling with the effort of trying not to cry. Sima reached around Mindy's shoulder, her hand on the back of her neck, under her hair. She put her other arm around Mindy, holding her up. And then Mindy started to cry. Sima held her, and Mindy cried and cried, her whole body shaking.

"You can't cry enough when you've lost someone you love," Mrs. Sampson said from her wheelchair. And the three of them sat with Mindy's tears, just tears.

There was a rumble overhead.

Mindy sniffled. "The giants are bowling," she said. "My father used to say that whenever there was a thunderstorm."

Mrs. Sampson smiled, her wrinkles deepening. "Girls believe anything their daddy tells them."

IT WAS MIDNIGHT BY THE time the CT was completed and the radiologist had arrived. Mindy stood at his elbow as he reviewed the scan. Sima stood by Mindy's other elbow, looking on.

"What do you see?" Mindy said. "Is it her spine?"

The radiologist put his face up close to the screen, and then he leaned back. "The spine is OK," he said. "No cord compression. Just a broken rib, alongside one of the vertebrae." He fingered the spot. Mindy and Sima both leaned in to see it. "A pathological fracture. Talk to Radiation in the morning. They'll give her a few treatments for the pain."

"Thanks for coming in," Mindy said.

"Thank you for getting her down here," he said. "These are the ones we don't want to miss."

18

Case Review

Sima opened the door to the House Staff Library on the sixth floor. No one was there. The interns and residents were across the hall in the conference room. The smell of pizza delivered by a drug rep for their noontime lecture permeated the corridor air. Sima was surprised Chief Danielson had scheduled the case review for this time of day. She wondered if Mindy had asked anyone to save her a piece of pizza, but then she'd have to explain why she wasn't attending the conference. It was likely Sima was going to miss lunch too.

She stepped inside the library and sat down in the closest chair. She and Mindy hadn't talked about Mr. Shtrom or the visit with the family or the case review, but both knew they had each received a letter. Sima expected Miss Armstrong to show up. She figured she was the one who instigated the whole thing. She was the one who had found Sima asleep in the library and reported her to Chief Danielson. She was the one who seemed most interested in seeing Sima go to medical school. Maybe she was trying to make Sima look good. Or maybe not.

She had arrived too early. She got up and paced the room. One side was windows halfway from the floor to the ceiling. The door side of the room was shelves of journals as high as the windows. In the middle of the room was a long, oval table. A few of the chairs on the side closest to the door jutted out. Sima stopped behind these outliers, pushed each one in, setting them right.

A whiff of pizza preceded Chief Danielson as he walked in. He might miss lunch too.

"Sima," he said. He set a large manila envelope down on the table and pulled out a chair, his back to the windows. "Have a seat."

Sima sat down again on the opposite side of the large table. The Chief seemed so far away and more serious than usual.

"Dr. Kahn should be here shortly," he said.

"Is anyone else coming?" Sima said.

"Not at this time," the Chief said.

More pizza scent and Mindy made her way in to join them. Her head down, she didn't make eye contact with Sima. She didn't seem to know where to look, where to go.

"Have a seat next to Sima," the Chief said. He stood up and walked to their side of the table. He opened the envelope the way he had done before and placed the pink progress note pages in front of them. "Do either of you know what we're here to talk about today?"

Both young women said nothing.

"Dr. Kahn, why don't you review the last note in these pages."

Mindy reached for the pages, turned them one by one, till she found the last entry. She took a minute to scan the page.

"Nothing is inaccurate," she said.

"That's what Sima said when I asked her to review it," the Chief said.

Sima hadn't told Mindy about her meeting with the Chief. She avoided Mindy's gaze.

"Is that your last note, Dr. Kahn?"

"It's the death note," Mindy said.

"Did you write that note?" he said.

Mindy stared at the page. She didn't look up.

"Is that your handwriting, Dr. Kahn?" He clicked his pen, tapped on the table.

He turned to Sima. "Did Dr. Kahn ask you to write this note?"

Sima never wrote anything in the hospital. How did the Chief know she had written it?

"No, sir. She was upset and I was trying to help."

"Miss Armstrong said you were very helpful with the family," the Chief said.

That was it. Miss Armstrong had changed her mind about Sima—she was meant to be a translator, not a doctor. Maybe she was right.

"I should have written the note," Dr. Kahn spoke up. "It was my responsibility."

"Yes, Dr. Kahn, you should have written the note," he said. "The chart is a legal document. Medical students write in charts, signed by an intern or a resident. Sima is an orderly. Orderlies don't write in charts. You should have written the note and signed it."

The final edict: Sima was an orderly.

They were both in trouble. She was trying to help and now Mindy's career was even more on the line than it had been. Chief Danielson would never write Sima a letter. She had lost her mentor, and her friend.

They sat at the table side by side, Orderly Sima and Mindy Kahn, MD, Intern, staring down at the death note. No eye contact. No words.

"Do you both understand?" the Chief said.

Sima didn't know what more was there to understand. She raised her eyes to the chief, in search of an answer. She heard the door open and the chief looked past her. And then Miss Armstrong was standing alongside the table where she and Mindy sat.

"Miss Armstrong has a few concerns," the Chief said.

He nodded at the tall, dark, hefty woman in white,

crispy clean cap neatly secured to her stiff brown hair. He motioned towards the end of the table closest to him. Head Nurse Armstrong pulled out a chair and sat down. She folded her hands in front of her.

What could Miss Armstrong want to know? Sima couldn't imagine.

The Chief cleared his throat and looked across the table at his charges. "Sima, Miss Armstrong tells me you gave Mr. Shtrom nitroglycerin that night," he said.

The woman had seen Sima hold the pill out to the old man.

"Miss Armstrong told me to get the bottle on the counter," Sima said. "I thought she told me to give him a pill and so I gave it to him." At least she had tried to give him the medicine that might ease his chest pain. She was an orderly. She did what she was told to do. She held the tiny tablet near his mouth, told him to take it under his tongue, sublingual. That's how it was given. That's what Miss Armstrong said to do. Sima had seen nurses do it all the time.

"Where was Dr. Kahn?" Chief Danielson asked.

Sima could feel Miss Armstrong's stare, heard her take a deep breath.

"I don't know," Sima said.

"Wasn't she in the on-call room, Sima?" Miss Armstrong said. "Didn't you tell me that?"

"I saw her in the on-call room earlier," Sima said. "She wasn't in the CCU when Mr. Shtrom needed the nitro, that's all I can say for sure." She didn't want to say any more. What did they want from her?

"Miss Armstrong is concerned about Dr. Kahn," the Chief said. "We both are. We need to know what happened."

She couldn't look at Miss Armstrong or the Chief. She could hear Mindy's breath getting faster. She didn't want to rat on her friend.

"You're a smart young woman, Sima," Chief Danielson said. "You could be an excellent doctor. I would like to be able to write you a letter of recommendation."

So this was it: lose a friend and her friend's future, or lose her own.

"Miss Armstrong said she paged you to CCU, Dr. Kahn," the Chief said. "Several times."

Mindy hadn't raised her eyes from the progress note. "I came when I could," she said.

"Sima, Miss Armstrong said she sent you to the on-call room to find Dr. Kahn," the Chief said. "Is that what you did?"

"I'm an orderly," Sima said.

"Did you go to the on-call room as Miss Armstrong asked you to?"

"Yes," Sima said. What else could she say?

"Was Dr. Kahn in the on-call room?"

"She was there."

"Did you inform her Miss Armstrong needed her in the CCU?"

"Her pager went off," Sima said.

"That isn't what I asked you," the Chief said.

Sima and Mindy side by side, their hands below the table, Miss Armstrong at the end on their left, her hands still folded in front of her. The faint smell of pizza in the air.

Chief Danielson stood. He passed behind Miss Armstrong to where the two young women sat. He reached over Mindy and collected the progress notes. He slid the pink pages into his large manila envelope, closed the clasp at the top. He tapped the envelope on the table.

"That will be all for now," he said. He opened the door to leave the library.

19

Hurry Up and Wait

Waiting was a New York City pastime Sima sometimes found hard to live with: waiting in line for a bus, for a subway train, to register for another course at Brooklyn College. Waiting in line to deposit her paycheck at the bank. Waiting for an elevator at the County. That's what being an orderly was all about. How many years of her life would she spend waiting? She found herself waiting for a seat in a cheap restaurant in Chinatown with her mother, and now her mother was nagging in Polish, pulling at Sima's sleeve to get her to ask the Chinese-speaking waitress if their table was ready yet.

These days she was willing to wait in line at the Korean corner market in her neighborhood to pay twice as much for a quart of milk as she would in the grocery store—where she'd have to wait even longer—because then her mother wouldn't be mad that she'd forgotten to pick up milk, again. At least she'd never have to wait to move her car to the opposite side of the street, since she didn't have a car. Mindy said she didn't live in the City because she lived in Brooklyn, not Manhattan. But Sima knew she was a New York City New Yorker when it came to cars: she didn't know how to drive, like so many life-long borough dwellers.

On days off when she occasionally ventured into the City alone, she saw people during rush hour wait to flag down an available cab. In the rain and the wind, on the kind of day that turns quick-draw umbrellas, five dollars a pop, inside out with no bus in sight, not even the Local that stops at every corner from Ninety-Sixth Street down to Alphabet City, Sima saw New Yorkers scramble and shuffle and fistfight their way into the one cab on Second Avenue: the business suit, the little old lady with purple hair, the banker babe in Brooks Brothers navy blue, red nails, red lipstick, and running shoes. Running shoes on women's feet all over NYC.

Waiting in line with her mother in lower Manhattan. She wished she could laugh.

It was their splurge. Once a month her mother wanted to get out of Brooklyn. Her mother now trusted Sima knew how to get around. They walked down the street together, headed for the B train at Kings Highway, six stops to DeKalb Avenue, then a change to the N train, to get off at Canal Street. Canal and Mott, the center of Chinatown.

From there, they could see Hester Street, a landmark for the old Jewish section of the Lower East Side. It was two blocks from Delancey Street and Ratner's, the *milkhik* dairy restaurant famous for blintzes, her mother's favorite. But today Sima's mother preferred a no-name hole-in-the-wall.

"You should be grateful your mama leaves the apartment with such a daughter," her mama said as they got off the train. She marched ahead to the nearest Chinese restaurant, the only one they ever went to, and stood there like a statue. "I slapped my daughter in shame."

"Enough is enough, Mama." The slap had been more than a month ago.

Once inside the restaurant, Sima put their name on a list. She handed her mother a menu.

"We could *sit* at Ratner's. Here we can order while we stand and wait." Sima never used to talk to her mother like this, but since the slap, she couldn't help herself. Every word was sarcastic. Maybe her mother was right to feel shame.

Her mother couldn't read the menu. She pointed to the pictures of what she wanted to eat.

"Beef and broccoli, fried rice?" Sima confirmed. "A bowl of wonton soup?" Her mother nodded. Nothing here was kosher but outside of the house, that was all right. There was no such thing as kosher in Poland, but this was America. And her mother had become an American Jew when it came to the few restaurants she and Sima could afford to visit. She drew a line at eating shrimp, which some American Jews chose to do outside of the house. It didn't matter that her mother didn't keep kosher now that she could. Her mother had no plans to ever eat shrimp.

Food was delivered to their table shortly after they sat down. It was a small, noisy place. Their table was tiny. And it was all they could do to slurp their soup in the silence between them. When the waitress removed their bowls, Sima filled her mother's plate with half the beef and broccoli and a generous portion of fried rice.

She wanted to tell her mother she was waiting to hear if Mindy would be kicked out of her internship. She wanted her mother to know she was waiting to talk with her mentor, her friend. She wanted a friend more than she wanted anything. But she knew if she told her mother that, her mother would get angry and they would speak even less than they ever did. Her mother only understood family and standing alongside each other, no matter what. What was a friend?

20

Heart Valve

It was his third or fourth bout of endocarditis since Sima and Mindy first met Mars Peabody on the Prison Ward almost ten months before. Each admission, he'd been plucked off the locked ward, tethered by the ankle to a bed on A71, and pampered by his very own intern. Each time, he'd left the hospital with the same bravado, managed to get out of Rikers, only to be back on the streets, shooting up all over again. Four weeks into another course of antibiotics, Mars Peabody's heart was failing.

Week by week, Sima had watched him grow tired of being sick. Laid out neatly now on his bedside table: a Tom Clancy paperback, the worn edges of its cover curled up off the first page, reading glasses, a slim white vase holding a single red rose. Mars had become a model patient. Like Mrs. Sampson, he was now someone Sima liked to take care of. Like Skinny and Miss Osborne and Alma Mae. She was more comfortable with these sick, poor people than she was with most of the medical staff. But if she became a doctor, she wouldn't be an outsider. She would be safe in a way her mama couldn't understand.

Sima rested a hand on Mars's buzz cut where it showed at the edge of the blue sterile drape that covered his face from his hairline down to the top of his neck. Stroked in one direction, his hair was soft, but it was bristly if approached from the top. He lay quietly under the drape that puffed up under the bulge of his nose with each exhale, his chest and arms also covered.

Mindy arrived at the bedside in a yellow cap and mask, gowned and gloved. No need to make eye contact with Sima for the task at hand. They hadn't worked a shift together for a few weeks. Mindy hadn't asked for help but Sima showed up at the right time to be there for her friend.

Mindy hovered over Mars, only wire rims and the end of an escaped curl showing. She pulled back the plunger of a small syringe fitted with a tiny twenty-five-gauge needle sunk into a bottle of lidocaine, and withdrew ten cc's. She had just disinfected Mars's neck with Betadine. In sterile gloves, she placed an index finger on the small area of exposed clean skin.

"You're going to feel a little prick, Mars," Mindy said. How many times Mindy had said this to patients, Sima couldn't imagine.

"I guess I'm only a little prick now," he said.

Finding a vein in an addict with endocarditis for a new IV every three days for six weeks. Mindy had months of experience now. The sores on Mars's arms and legs had healed, but he was still an impossible stick.

⁖ The drape moved.

"You have to lie still." Mindy's voice was muffled through her mask.

"My nose itches," Mars said.

Sima lifted a corner of the drape, peeked in at Mars, and scratched the tip of his nose.

"To the right a little," Mars said. "Yeah, that's it. Ahhh."

They waited for the lidocaine to take effect.

Mindy's breath escaped at the top of her mask, fogging her glasses.

"Let me wipe those," Sima said. She reached to lift Mindy's wire rims off her nose.

"I can see," Mindy said. "Put my glasses back on before the lidocaine wears off."

"You could say, 'Please,'" Mars said from under the drape. "But you're one of the guys."

"There are only six women out of thirty interns," Mindy said. "You have to become one of them." She stood gowned and gloved and masked and capped over her patient.

After a few minutes, Mindy removed the cover from

a needle and lightly danced the tip on the skin where she had injected the lidocaine.

"Do you feel this?" she said.

"Don't feel a thing," Mars said from under his drape.

She put the needle tip into the skin a little deeper. "Feel this?"

"Don't feel a thing, doctor."

Mindy settled one hand on Mars's draped shoulder. With the other, she stuck a wide-bore needle into her patient's neck, her thumb covering the open end to keep Mars's blood from gushing out. She pushed an introducer in through the needle, now deep in the large hidden vein. She attached IV tubing connected to a bag of fluid and opened the valve. Clear liquid ran through the plastic, disappearing beneath black skin. She lifted the drape over Mars's shoulder and taped the line against his neck and down his arm. She removed the drape from her patient's face and the mask from her own. There were dents in her skin where the elastic of the cap had dug into her forehead. She rubbed at the dents with the back of her hand.

There were no wrinkles around Mars's eyes, only a few on his forehead. He sat up in bed, hands on his knees, cross-legged like a Buddha. A Buddha with one leg chained to a hospital bed. The skin on his arms and legs was smooth and clear.

He spoke softly. "Everybody wants to be white," Mars said.

"What are you talking about?" Mindy pulled off her gown and gloves, bunched them into a ball. It seemed as though she couldn't get away from the bedside fast enough.

"You're a Jew, too, ain't you, doc?" he said. "No Jew woman ever going to be white, is all I'm saying," he said. "The white man thinks everybody wants to be just like him. But no immigrant ever going to be white, either. Like Sima here."

"You think you can change who you are?" Mindy stuffed the used items into a garbage bag. "You're a drug addict caught stealing and who got sick. Many times."

"I'm different now." He put his hand over his heart. "Mars Peabody, drug addict gone straight."

"Your heart is failing and you've got a chain around your ankle," Mindy said.

Mindy spoke with the same kind of sarcasm Sima now used with her mother.

Change wasn't easy for anyone.

The hospital cop moved Mars's cuff from the bed to a wheelchair so Sima could take him for an echocardiogram. She pushed the wheelchair with one hand, the IV pole with the other; the hospital cop trailed behind Mars, model patient or not.

"Why do I need another scan?" Mars said. "Dr. Kahn already said I need a new heart valve, didn't she?"

"The surgeons like to be sure."

It wasn't Sima's job to explain tests to patients, but they often asked her. She wasn't going to tell Mars the surgeons were dragging their feet. Mindy said they hated replacing valves in addicts just to see them show up six months later, sick again, just like Mars himself before his big reform.

Mars pulled a smudged brown leather wallet out of the pocket of his bathrobe. He fingered an irregular tear in the leather, gently, like he was touching a woman's skin. He opened the wallet and held it up for Sima to see the photographs of a little boy with light brown skin and green eyes.

"My boy," he said. "Hair so smooth, like his mother's."

Sima's eyes were glued to the boy's face, his light skin and green eyes.

"Look at that smile. Them ears and teeth." Mars ran his finger along the boy's lips. "He lost the front ones when he was two." He handed the photograph to Sima.

She remembered putting her two front teeth under the pillow for the tooth fairy when she was five. Mama got mad at Papa because he left Sima a big piece of chocolate halavah.

"That's young to lose baby teeth."

"He got kicked." The corners of Mars's mouth turned down. He tapped one of his slippers on the footrest of the wheelchair. "His mother," he said. "She was piece of work. I gave her everything a street man could, but she always wanted something more, something different."

Sima looked at Mars and then at the smile on the little boy.

Mars closed his eyes. "It was me who kicked him," he said, as though she had forced it out of him. "I wanted to kick *her*. She told me she wanted me out of her life and his, too. I was dark; they were light. I got so fucking mad." Mars grabbed at the handcuff on his wrist, pulled on it until the silver metal dug a line into his skin. "My foot flew out—I kicked the boy. He was standing right there beside her."

Sima handed the photograph back to Mars.

"There was blood everywhere, and the little guy was crying." Mars shrugged. "She was screaming like I killed the kid. I just knocked out two teeth." He put the wallet away.

"Where's he now?"

Mars shrugged.

Sima doubted Mars's son would even recognize his father, that she would recognize her *own* father if he were to show up alive after all these years. All she remembered of him was his face scrunched up, lying on the poster for

Oklahoma! That and his image in the one photograph in which she stood holding his hand, her mother on the other side of him. They all wore long, heavy coats and hats that covered their ears. Her father's face was so small in the photograph that she could barely make out his features. All the faces were small.

21

Gurney Ride

Mars lay on a gurney in front of the elevator, his trusty hospital cop, Officer Nelson, at his side. A black beret was perched on Mars's bristly-soft hair, shaved flat by the hospital barber every week, as regular as his blood draws. His legs were crossed at the ankles, his toes covered with blue foam-rubber hospital slippers. Except for the hospital pajamas and the cuff on his right ankle, Mars looked as though he were lounging at the beach.

"Where'd you get that hat?" Sima said.

A big white-toothed grin came across Mars's face. He put both hands behind his head. "Old friend gave it to me," he said.

Sima pressed the UP button a third time. "Old drug addict friend?"

"One of the oldest," Mars coughed and then propped himself on his elbows, breathy. "He's fifty-seven years young."

"I've never seen a drug addict that old."

"Sima, my young friend, there's lots of things you never seen," Mars laugh-coughed.

His chart rested alongside him on the gurney. Sima flipped it open, something an orderly wasn't supposed to do, and fingered the face sheet. "Says here you're thirty-seven."

Mars said, "I met Bug Man when I was fifteen, just starting out on the streets."

Nelson, the slowest moving cop at the County, stood up from where he'd been leaning against the wall on the other side of the elevator. Nelson was also the oldest and the fattest but size, age, and speed didn't matter for taking watch over Mars now that he was reformed. And sick as he was.

"That Bug Man Bruno you talking about?" Nelson said. "I thought he kicked the bucket ages ago."

"Bruno's been clean for seven years now. He's living the good life, shacked up with a nice senorita."

"I thought he would go to his grave with needles sticking out every which way. He practically lived here, he was sick so much," Nelson said, moving closer to Mars.

Sima fingered the UP button a few more times. "He quit the way you did, Mars?" she said. "Another reformed citizen?"

Mars rattled the chain around his ankle against the gurney rail. "I had to get locked up in here to get straight," he said. "Bug Man, he just quit. Cold turkey. He could feel the bug, the creep of drugs all over his body when it was wanting. That's why they called him Bug." He straightened his beret as though he were checking himself out in a mirror for a special lady. "He's coming all the way from Mexico," he said. "He's going to find Derek, my son. He's going to bring him here to see his old man." Mars rubbed his chest. "To see his daddy."

Nelson bent in toward Mars. "I didn't know you had a son."

"Man, get out of my face," Mars said. He put his hand up to Nelson's chest and pushed him away. Nelson grabbed for Mars's arm, but Mars yanked the arm back out of reach. "You got bad breath like them dogs in the TV commercials. Go get yourself some Milk-Bones. Clean them puppies up."

Nelson rolled his eyes and leaned away. "Milk-Bones," he said. "Hmph. You reformed addicts is worse than the guys still copping for a fix. You think you're better than other dogs 'cause you kicked."

Mars started to cough.

"Sit up," Sima said to Mars. "Nelson, help me sit him up." Mars was wheezing.

"Breathe slowly," Sima said. There was no red EMERGENCY button in the hallway. "Where's the damn elevator?" She elbowed Nelson. "Get the oxygen tank."

Nelson bent his rickety knees. He strong-armed the

tank onto the gurney next to Mars's legs from the shelf underneath where it sat ready for moments like this one.

"Tubing," Sima said. She grabbed the clear plastic bag draped around the neck of the tank. She pulled out the length of tubing with the nose prongs and stretched the elastic band over the top of Mars' head. She placed the prongs into Mars's nose, attached the other end to the tank and turned the nozzle on. Oxygen whooshed out the valve and through the tubing. Nelson helped Sima raise the back of the gurney as high as it would go. They propped Mars up against his pillow.

Mars coughed up a tiny speck of bright red blood and then a tablespoonful. The blood dripped down his chin and onto his hospital johnny. A bit of the red stuff splattered, just missing Sima's hand on the gurney rail. He coughed again, and a speck of his blood landed on the side rail nearest Nelson.

The elevator door opened.

Miss Lawrence stood up from her chair. "This patient doesn't look good," she said. "Got an emergency here. Everybody off."

They filed off quickly: a lab tech white-coated neck to knee, two shiny-faced med students in their short white jackets, a handful of relatives waving orange VISITOR cards.

Nelson was at the foot-end of the gurney, Sima at the head. Nelson barely got his big old butt across the threshold before Miss Lawrence pulled out the stop button and the elevator door closed behind him. Mars was wheezing, more blood drooled down his chin.

"Got to go directly to the ER—express." Sima blurted out.

"We ain't got no express here, Sima," Miss Lawrence said. "We just won't make no stops." Then she got on the telephone on the elevator wall and was talking to someone in the ER. "We got a very sick man here on this elevator."

Nelson leaned into the back wall of the elevator. Sima had one hand on Mars's back and her other on his shoulder. "Try to breathe slowly," she said. His lips were blue.

The elevator door opened, and Sima heard the doctors running down the hall toward them. The side rails of the gurney slipped out of Sima's hands as they rolled Mars out, as quickly as possible, to the ER. A minute later, a voice on the overhead called out, "Code blue in the ER."

Once the code ended, that's when they usually paged Sima. After the ten rounds of epi and bicarb and three pushes of lidocaine, when the blood gas was dark purple instead of red. When the blood gas came back blue for the second or third time, the head of the code team gave the final command: time of death.

But Sima was already there this time when she heard the senior resident call it. One doctor and then a few appeared around the edges of the curtain, their heads low and heavy.

The white sheet was pulled up to Mars's neck, his hair tidy, his skin clean: ready to see Derek and Bug Man. His forehead had no wrinkles now, nor the sides of his mouth down to his fuzzy chin, where he had been trying to grow a goatee. His lips were blue.

"Mars." Sima lay a hand on his shoulder, which wasn't yet stiff under the sheet. At the head of the bed, the ER nurse lifted the sheet from below Mars's chin. She raised it over his face, his blue lips gone forever. His forehead, his nose, his chin, a silhouette of white.

"The surgeons waited too long," Sima said. "It was his only chance."

The nurse smoothed a long wrinkle in the sheet over Mars's chest. "I'm afraid our friend here had used up his chances." She lifted the edge of the sheet and covered Mars's fingertips.

"But he gave it all up," Sima said. "He wanted to see his son."

Sima peeked under the sheet, pulled it aside. An alcohol pad stuck to Mars's chest near his left nipple.

"Cover the body, Sima," the nurse lowered her voice. "We got a room full of patients here." She reached for the sheet and covered Mars again, his nipples, the curlicue hairs on his chest, the buzz cut.

"His hat," Sima said. She scanned the gurney, the floor. The trash barrel by the bed was filled to the brim with bloodied blue pads.

"Let me help you push him out into the hallway," the nurse said. She unlocked the wheels of the gurney, situated herself at the head end, and set the deathbed in motion.

The intermittent screech of gurney wheels and the squish of soft-soled shoes drowned out any other sounds as the two of them pushed the body toward the elevator, where Miss Lawrence held the door open. One last shove and the gurney was inside.

Sima listened to the fan in the back corner pushing stuffy air around and around. Elevator lady air, orderly air, dead man air. There was nothing like the smell of dead man air. Or the vision of a dead man dressed for the morgue. Birth and death: always draped in white.

The fan was stuck in one position. The air blew straight at the bundled chart, moved one corner of the top page and then lifted them all. Page after page, one edge and then the whole sheaf up in the air. Mars Peabody's last days flew off his crotch. One page hit the back wall of the elevator, another lapped against the handrail, one grazed Miss Lawrence's elbow.

"Damn fan," Miss Lawrence said.

Sima got down on her knees to gather the pages.

"Hope he went fast," Miss Lawrence said. "Ain't no good death but a fast one."

"In the end it was," Sima said. She collected Mars's days, page by page, and placed them back in order, from the face sheet to the ER admission to the daily progress notes, lab tests, order sheets, and consultations by half the specialists at the County.

The elevator door opened to the tunnel.

"There you go, Sima," Miss Lawrence said.

Mars was dead. He was a dead father, like Mindy's father, and Sima's own. And Mr. Shtrom.

PAST THE MUMMY PIPES, HISS and steam, the buzz of fluorescence. The giants bowling overhead. The bumping and screeching that meant life.

The yellow light in the tunnel usually made everything blurry, and tonight it was worse. Sima was crying. No more elevator rides. No more gurneys to push. Mars, Mr. Shtrom, Mindy's father. Her baby brother. No more dead bodies. She had been the one to find her father dead but then her mother said she was too young to go the funeral.

She heard Tunnel Guy before she saw him coming down the long hallway, a dark face, a spiky dark head bopping up and down, the sound of the radio blasting out through his headphones.

Tunnel Guy stopped at the foot end of the gurney.

"I've got a dead man here," Sima said.

"You got a lumpy gurney covered with a white sheet," Tunnel Guy said, his curly head still moving with the beat.

"Show a little respect," Sima said.

"That's a black man's line," he said, opened his eyes wide. "You ain't no black man."

"This is a black man," Sima said. "A dead black man."

"Once you're dead, you're dead," Tunnel Guy said.

Sima was close enough this time but she still didn't see a name tag on this ghoul. "You're *maintenance.* You're not the one who delivers them to the morgue."

"Morgue is that way," he said. He pointed to the hallway behind her. Then he strutted past the gurney in the direction he had been pointing. He disappeared into the cloud of mummy pipe steam.

THE DEATH CERTIFICATE OFFICE DIDN'T know Mars was dead yet. They hadn't called Mindy down to sign the death certificate. Mars hadn't listed anyone as next of kin; he hadn't even known his son was alive until he got a letter from Bug Man. Mindy now had to face a relative she had never met before, with the patient already dead. Mindy asked Sima to be there with her.

Late May, almost June, and not yet summer in Brooklyn, late afternoon. Mindy and Sima stopped in the middle of the hallway. They let a gurney go by and then made their way to the wall of chairs across from the Nurses' Station on A71.

An older black man with gray-white kinky hair sat at the close end. A much younger male, a lanky teenager with dark brown wavy hair and lighter skin, was posted nearer to the hallway, watching all the traffic: patients being pushed in wheelchairs and on gurneys, interns and residents walking back and forth from the Nurses' Station, writing orders and answering pages, heading off into the big ward or disappearing into the charting area.

Sima and Mindy approached. The older man stood up.

"I'm Dr. Kahn," Mindy said to the teenager she assumed to be Derek, "your father's doctor." She held her hand out toward him.

The older man put an arm around the younger. "This here's my buddy's son, Derek. I'm Bruno Bailey, but they call me the Bug Man," he said. He nudged Derek. "Shake hands with the doctor, son."

Mindy reached out again.

"Go on," Bug Man said.

Derek barely lifted he eyes. He stretched an arm toward Mindy, and the two shook hands.

"We've heard a lot about you," Sima said to Bug Man. Then she turned to Derek. "Your father showed us a picture of you when you were a little boy."

Sima saw Mars's big white teeth in the mouth of the teenager. When Derek stopped smiling, she noticed he was fidgeting with a button on his shirt. The button was hanging by a thread, about to fall off.

"Can I see my father?"

"Let's sit down a minute," Mindy said. She led them back to the row of chairs. She stood until they sat down, and then she sat next to Derek. Sima remained standing.

Mindy pulled patient note cards out of her coat's breast pocket, tapped the cards against her knee. Then she put the cards into a side pocket. She cleared her throat, closed her eyes for a second, and then opened them.

"I don't know what your father wrote in his letter," Mindy said. She folded her hands in her lap. "Sima here helped him write it."

Sima smiled though she wanted to cry. Mars had done lots of bad things. But she had stayed late one night to read the final version of the letter. She'd bought a stamp for the envelope and the letter went out in the hospital mail the next day.

"He sent the letter to me," Bug Man said. "He wrote that he had a really good doctor. A Jewish lady doctor from Boston. Must be you he was talking about." He smiled at Mindy.

"He had a bad infection in his heart from using drugs," Mindy said. "Did you know about that, Derek?"

Derek turned to Bug Man. "You said he quit drugs."

Bug Man's eyes went wide. "That's what got him into the hospital," he said. "He got clean after he was here."

"The infection wasn't going away," Mindy said. "It damaged one of his heart valves."

Derek yanked at the loose button on his shirt and the button made a tiny sound as it landed on the floor.

Mindy picked the button up and placed it in Derek's hand. "Your father was very sick."

Derek turned to Bug Man. "Can I see him now?"

Mindy put a hand on Derek's shoulder. He shrugged away from her touch.

"I came all the way from Virginia to see my father," he said. "I want to see my father."

Mindy kept her eyes on Derek. "Your father's heart gave out last night," she said. "We did everything we could. But his mitral valve tore. His lungs filled with blood. He couldn't breathe, and then his heart stopped. I'm so sorry to tell you this. He died last night."

"Mars is dead?" Bug Man said.

"My father died?" Derek said.

"We did everything we could," Mindy said. "The infection in his heart was very bad."

Derek pulled further away from Mindy and stood up.

He walked back and forth in front of the chairs, and then he stepped toward the Nurses' Station a few feet away. A young nurse was delivering an elderly woman in a wheelchair to the ward. The old woman looked at Derek and smiled. Derek raised his arms over his head, then covered his face with his hands.

"But I got here, Bruno brought me here," Derek cried. "He said I had to come."

Mindy moved closer to the tall young man. She rested a gentle hand on his arm again.

In his face, Sima glimpsed the five-year-old boy from Mars's photo.

"He really wanted to see you again," Mindy said.

22

Bridges

Sima liked to think about how bridges kept one side of a city away from its other side. How they separated the hills from the flats, the old parts from the new. Kept big buildings away from little buildings, business buildings away from those where people lived. San Francisco, San Diego, St. Louis, Tampa–St. Petersburg. Portland, Oregon. Paris, France. New York, New York.

But what separated people was more than geography. East Side, West Side, Uptown, Downtown, the Lower East Side, the Upper West Side. History. It was not just where your parents were born but where they went to college, if they had the opportunity to go to college at all. If English was their native language. Vegetarian or meat eater, couch potato or marathon runner, walker or Rollerblader or cyclist vying for road space in Central Park on Saturday and Sunday mornings when the weather was dry and not too cold.

Many who lived in the City would never consider riding a bike any more than others would ever consider eating at McDonald's. The rich and the middle class lived *here* in New York City, in Manhattan, the center of the universe. And everyone else lived where they could. All anyone had to do to tell the difference was to stand on a busy street corner and notice who was driving the cabs and the buses, selling the newspapers, or sitting on a curb with a hand out, trying not to get stepped on.

The Brooklyn Bridge, the Manhattan Bridge, the Williamsburg Bridge, the Queensboro Bridge, the Triborough Bridge.

Puerto Ricans, Cubans, Koreans, Indians, West Indians, Pakistanis, Samoans, West Africans, WASPs, Hispanics, and Jews—Hasidic or not. Old Chinese bent from an ancient history of heavy loads.

Sima noticed there was something about having the choice to cross a body of water by car instead of by subway or bus that made a person's accent change. At least in this city.

Mindy said Sima didn't live in the City; she lived in Brooklyn. Sima had driven into Manhattan only once, through the Brooklyn–Battery Tunnel. Three o'clock in the morning, but there had been too much snow falling to for her to see the tall buildings lit up on the other end, the water along the docks. The Statue of Liberty in the harbor, her arm raised to the Big Apple sky. Sima thought it would be hard to die the way Mindy's father had, all alone. It rarely happened that way at the County. All those white coats and running shoes.

AFTER ROUNDS WITH THE MEDICAL students one afternoon, Sima stood silently alongside Chief Danielson. She cleared her throat, cleared it again. Chief Danielson turned to Sima and waited.

"Why did you assign Dr. Kahn to the CCU right after her father died of a heart attack?" She blurted the words out, with that tone her mother hated so much. It was the only way to say what she had to say.

Chief Danielson put his hands in the pockets of his long white chief coat and rocked on his heels. He peered down at his shoes, then regarded Sima.

"That's a good question," he said. "An honest and a brave one. Thank you for asking it."

ON HER DOUBLE SHIFT THE second week of June, Sima saw Mindy running to the lab, to the ER, to answer this page and that one. Mindy's senior resident was busy helping four sub-interns, fourth-year medical students learning to do the work of interns. Every procedure the subs did had to be supervised, every order co-signed. That left Mindy pretty much on her own for the night. But by the end of the month, Mindy would become a resident herself, so she didn't need much help anymore. She had survived the case review, she had made it through a year at the County as a psych rotator. Sima thought maybe Mindy would stay in Medicine.

Sima was called to A71 to transport Mindy's admission for an X-ray the ER had forgotten to take. Mindy was carrying the code beeper for the senior resident while he escaped from his subs to take a quick shower. Sima scheduled all her double shifts when Mindy was on call now. They were friends again. Mindy had convinced Sima to sign up for English composition in summer school. She thought Sima should graduate for sure.

"Another night in the trenches," Mindy said. "Good to have my personal orderly at my side."

As Mindy helped Sima move the patient out of bed and into a wheelchair, the code beeper went off. A snippet of white sheet from the bed got caught in one wheel of the chair, and the sheet tugged hard on the patient's leg. The woman moaned.

Sima released the sheet as gently as she could while Mindy looked down at the pager to see what ward the code was on.

Sima said, "Just go."

Mindy ran.

At the end of the hallway, Mindy turned and called out, "Sima, come with me!"

Sima was supposed to take the patient to X-ray. Instead she was pushing the wheelchair to the side of the hallway and chasing Mindy down the hallway.

"Hey!" the patient yelled, but Sima didn't look back.

Sima caught up with Mindy at the elevators. Mindy smashed hard on the red EMERGENCY button. When the elevator door didn't open, Mindy headed to the stairwell, Sima at her heels.

No air. No light. Dried urine, running shoes sticking to the floor, three flights down.

Sima could barely keep Mindy in sight, Mindy's feet were so fast. She didn't falter as she pushed through the door to A41, three floors down from her usual ward.

"Where's the code?" Mindy asked the head nurse there.

"The Isolation Room," the nurse said.

Outside the room was a cart topped with a pile of rubber gloves and a box of blue paper masks. Mindy stuffed her arms into a gown, stretched a glove onto each hand. She grabbed two masks.

"Here." Mindy handed a mask to Sima. "Grab a gown." She gave Sima a pair of gloves.

"Where's the rest of the team?" Sima said.

"I don't know." Mindy tied the mask around the back of her curly head and pushed the door into the Isolation Room. Sima followed.

And then it was slow motion.

Mindy in her wrinkled yellow gown, hair sticking out around the mask, stepped to the head of the bed, to the right side of a patient she had never seen before. She leaned down, put her face up close to the patient's mouth listening, felt for a pulse at the neck.

"His pulse is weak. He's not breathing," she said. "We need to bag him."

Mindy grabbed the Ambu bag from the crash cart. She lifted the patient's chin out and up, and covered his mouth with the breathing bag to make a good seal.

"You bag him," Mindy said to Sima. "I'll pump."

Slow motion. A few seconds felt like an hour.

Then Sima was at the head of the bed next to Mindy. It was just the two of them. She didn't remember pulling her gloves on, but there they were, on her hands. Mindy's gloved hands were there, over Sima's showing her how to keep a good seal on the Ambu bag, how to squeeze air into the patient's lungs. The patient's chest moved up with each squeeze moving air in, then down as the air came back out.

Mindy felt again for a pulse. "No pulse." And then Mindy made a fist and thumped the center of the patient's chest. She laced her fingers together, the heel of one hand on top of the other. Mindy leaned hard into the patient's chest with her whole weight.

"One-one thousand, two-one thousand, three-one thousand, four-one thousand, five-one thousand." Mindy pumped and Sima squeezed. Again and again.

The door to the Isolation Room opened, and the intern from A41 pushed his way in.

"Hook him up to the EKG," Mindy said, her voice loud, deep.

"Do we have a rhythm?" Mindy said, still pumping. Sima kept squeezing air.

"Yes," the A41 intern said. "But it's not sinus."

"What is it?" Mindy asked, but A41 intern just stared at the EKG.

"You pump," Mindy said to the intern.

The intern took Mindy's place and started to pump. Mindy moved to the EKG machine.

One minute. Felt like ten.

A race. In slow motion.

"It's v-tach," Mindy said. "We've got to shock him." She picked up the paddles from the top of the Crash Cart. "Everybody stand back," she said.

Sima and the A41 intern stood back from the bed. Mindy placed the paddles on the patient's chest and pushed two red buttons. The patient's whole body arched off the bed. "Keep pumping and bagging!" Mindy shouted.

"We've got a rhythm!" The head nurse was in the Isolation Room now, too.

Mindy turned to look at the EKG. "He's in sinus," she said. "Do we have a pulse?"

"Yes," the A41 intern said.

"Stop pumping. We need to get a line into him," Mindy said.

The A41 intern stopped pumping, grabbed an IV catheter, and got working on the line.

Mindy moved to the patient's head. "I'm going to tube him," she said. "He's not breathing."

"Shouldn't we wait for anesthesia or the senior?" the A41 intern said.

Mindy took the laryngoscope from the top of the crash cart where the head nurse stood.

"Stop bagging him," she said. Sima stepped back and Mindy leaned over the patient at the head of the bed. She rested the laryngoscope on the patient's chest. Then with her left hand, she lifted the man's chin higher in the air. She picked up the laryngoscope again in her right hand.

Then, as if she had been doing it her whole life, Mindy slipped the laryngoscope into the patient's mouth and down into his throat. The head nurse handed her an endotracheal tube and she inserted the tube into the patient's trachea. She removed the stylet, then the scope. She inflated the cuff on the side of the tube and attached the end of the tube to the Ambu bag as Sima had seen done so many times.

"Bag him," Mindy said. Sima squeezed the bag and watched as Mindy fitted her stethoscope into her ears and placed the bell on the patient's chest to listen for breath sounds.

"It's in," Mindy said. "Keep bagging."

Then suddenly the patient coughed. He opened his eyes and coughed again. The muscles and veins in his neck bulged. He pushed the Ambu bag out of Sima's hands, and then he grabbed the tube in his throat. One, two, three. He yanked the tube out of his throat and gave a huge cough.

Sima, Mindy, the A41 intern, and the head nurse stood by the bed and watched the man breathe on his own.

The A41 intern reached out to pat Mindy's arm. "Good save," he said.

The head nurse nodded, her blue mask moving up and down. "Good job, Dr. Kahn."

Sima had never seen a patient survive a code. Mindy's first code as the one in charge. And still an intern. And the patient was alive.

SIMA AND MINDY DROVE INTO the City. They took the Brooklyn Bridge this time. It was June and wasn't dark yet at the end of their workday. Sima watched the buildings in Manhattan just begin to light up, reflecting over the waterfront, the bows of boats, and the surrounding boroughs.

Sima noted a small tear in the elbow of her old top. She liked the blouse Mindy was wearing. It was loose, with a scoop neck and horizontal gray pinstripes. The bottom edge came just to the waistline of her black skirt. It was airy and cool, perfect for a warm New York City night in early June. Long silver earrings with tiny dots of red and green stone hung from Mindy's ears. Her hair was not post-call kinky but smooth-curly and still smelled of a shower. It was the first time Sima had smelled Mindy so clean, the first time they had gone into the City together for the fun of it.

"The last time we—" Sima said before stopping herself. She had been about to say, *The last time we went into the City together was the night we went to your father's*, but she didn't want to spoil the good feeling in the air.

"The last time we what?" Mindy said. She pulled her left arm inside the car, rolled the window up halfway, and turned on the radio.

"Never mind," Sima said and rolled her window up, too.

Mindy's head bopped to the familiar notes just beginning on the radio. "'Rubber Soul'!" she said. "My favorite

Beatles song." She reached for the dial and turned it louder. The Beatles' chiming voices filled the car, singing of unforgettable faces, of wanting all the world to see.

"Rubber Soul," Sima said. "I know every word on that album."

Mindy shrugged. She smiled and sang along.

Sima had never considered that American-born girls her age might like the Beatles as much as she did. Well, almost as much. Sima joined Mindy in singing at the top of her voice.

When the tune ended and Mindy turned the radio down again, Sima reached out over the Rebel's long, flat front seat. "You know," she poked Mindy's elbow, "'Rubber Soul' isn't the name of a song."

Mindy was still tipping her head side to side, tapping one hand on the steering wheel. She gave Sima a short but penetrating look. "You always have to get it right," she said.

"Well," Sima said, "The truth is the truth."

"So, 'Rubber Soul' is not a song," Mindy said. She frowned for a couple of seconds, her face long, her mouth down, and then she turned to Sima and smiled.

"We all need a rubber soul!" Sima shouted, "So we can bounce back!"

"Bounce back," Mindy said. "I like that!"

I'm rubber, and you're glue. What you say bounces off me

and sticks to you too. Like Teflon and Ronald Reagan. Moral crises, years of lies, deceit, torture. Having a rubber soul meant you could bounce back from anything.

"There could be a black market for rubber souls," Sima said, "or maybe the Greek coffee trucks could sell them. Coffee, bagels, rubber souls!" she called, her hands up to her mouth like a megaphone. "Get your rubber soul here! Fresh from the factory. No delivery charge. Two for a dollar. Special today. Buy one for that lovely lady. No extra charge."

Bounce back when life dents you. The dimples popped out again, the edges rounded smooth.

Mindy glanced at Sima. "Black market for rubber souls," she said. "Ha. And I thought *I* was sleep deprived." They both laughed.

The end of the bridge was just up ahead. They were over the river into the warm rush-hour New York City summer night. Twilight. Not quite light anymore but not quite dark, either. The City with a capital *C*.

"I never saw a cardiac arrest where the patient sat up and talked," Sima said.

"It happens sometimes," Mindy said. "People make it."

"Not very often at the County," Sima said. "You were really on. It was pretty cool."

"You did as much as I did," Mindy said.

"No way," Sima said. "I just did what you told me to do."

"He was your save as much as mine," Mindy said.

Save. Money in the bank. A big sale at Pottery Barn, at Zabar's, at the Times Square ticket booth, places Sima could only dream about. A big sale at Macy's—her mother could buy new towels. Save a life. Sima had never seen a dead person come back to life.

"Why did ask me to come with you to the code?" Sima said.

"I knew you could help me," she said. "You've been at almost as many codes as I have."

"I usually get called when the code is over," Sima said.

"I knew the A41 intern was out to lunch, the head nurse, too. She never does anything except page the intern on call for every little thing she never wants to do."

"My fingers got sore bagging him," Sima said. "They're still sore."

"I wanted you there," Mindy said.

"Chief Danielson was smiling this morning," Sima said.

Mindy tilted her head toward her side window. "He does that sometimes," she said.

"He hasn't smiled at you since November."

"Slap on the back, ready to hand you a cigar," Mindy said. "'You're one of the boys now.' Take that damn English class and you're going to be one of us too, a good one."

"Chief Danielson said he'd write me a letter."

Sima rolled down her window again, stuck her lifesaving fingers out into the warm air. It was time to tell her mother she was about to become a college graduate. One course to go. And she would have a letter of recommendation to medical school. She would make tea and sit down with her mother. If she told her with conviction, with her truest feeling and without sarcasm, her mother would listen. She was her mother's only child. She was all her mother had. She was her mother. And Sima was *her* daughter. That would never change. Her *prosta* mother would be proud.

Mindy sat up higher in her seat. "What happened to that patient you left in the wheelchair?"

"The patient wheeled herself down to the Nurses' Station in a fit," Sima said. "Nurse Armstrong heard about it. She said she was going to report me. But then she smiled."

Mindy laughed. They laughed together.

Mindy would push Sima to apply to medical school, she needed her friend to do that.

"She has a better sense of humor than when I first started working there," Sima said.

"Hey, I've never eaten real Polish food," Mindy said. "Let's go to a Polish restaurant."

"Yeah?" Sima said.

"East Village," Mindy said. "There must be a place there."

"The Kiev," Sima said. "Let's go to the Kiev." She'd bring home a babka for tea.

"No better place to watch rubber souls in action than the East Village."

They got off the FDR at the tip of Manhattan, the City, where it was only a few blocks from one side of the island to the other, and headed to the Kiev. They spent the next two hours stuffing themselves on Eastern European delicacies: blintzes, borscht, and babka, kasha varnishkes, and thick slices of golden challah.

23

Museum Beads

Sima saw Mindy standing by the door to the six-bed Female Room. Mrs. Sampson was back again, this time for shortness of breath, and Mindy stood there, intern tall. Her hair was post-Kiev and pre-call clean, her curls still holding their own against the night. She wasn't wearing her short white jacket on her last night on call as an intern. In a few days, she'd become a resident.

The short Chinese oncology fellow in charge of Mrs. Sampson's chemo marched out of the room with Mrs. Sampson's chart under his arm. He brushed Mindy's shoulder on his way out.

"What did you say to Mrs. Sampson?" Sima heard Mindy ask him.

From where Sima stood across the hall, she could see Mrs. Sampson's long face, her eyes closed, her head down.

The oncology fellow slowed his step, just enough to glance at Mindy over his shoulder. He wore a long coat because he was a fellow, which meant he was closest to being an attending. "Patient have breast cancer," he said. "Metastases all over her lungs. She will die soon."

Mindy grabbed Dr. Shum's sleeve. "You can't talk to her like that," she said.

Dr. Shum turned to Mindy, and Sima saw the whole of him, shaped like a block—block body, block limbs, block head.

"I am the oncologist," he said. "That is my job. Must tell patient the truth." Eye to eye with Mindy, no smile, no frown, just the facts.

"But that's not the way to do it," Mindy said.

"All patients are upset when they will die," he said.

"You should have told her when her family was here," Mindy said. "Her daughter."

"Can't wait for daughter," he said. "Must see other patients."

"You can help this patient find a little hope." Mindy wouldn't let go of his sleeve. "That's part of your job."

He stood so still. He turned his block body out of Mindy's reach, and walked away.

Sima tried to get Mindy's attention, but Mindy followed Dr. Shum down the hallway, still ranting at him to no avail.

The truth, whatever that was. How to tell the truth. That patients with bad breasts like Mrs. Sampson, bad hearts like Mr. Shtrom, bad valves like Mars Peabody, with body parts that wouldn't do their share of the living anymore, would die. No matter what the doctors did. No matter how much chemotherapy or how many cardiac meds and IVs and antibiotics. No matter how many or how few times a nurse or a doctor came to their bedside and felt for their pulse. Whether the doctors made mistakes or not. Whether they told the truth or not. Whether they managed to leave the slightest bit of hope. They would die. Some sooner than later.

Sima stood in the doorway of the Female Room, on the same squares of linoleum where Mindy had just stood. Mrs. Sampson's long sewing fingers were spread out over her chest on the side where the breast was gone. Mrs. Sampson, only one day back but already with pillow hair. The whites of her eyes were red, her face was wet.

"Mrs. Sampson," Sima said.

Thin old-lady fingers moved from her chest to the bed. Sima studied the thimble finger, the middle one, on Mrs. Sampson's right hand. It moved more than the other fingers—it was the finger in charge. The fingers needed something to do, some sewing. But there was no sewing, no small plaid button-down shirt, and the fingers only patted the mattress. Sima sat down on the side of Mrs. Sampson's bed. Her bony knees bumped up under the sheet, the outline of her covered legs was so thin.

"Sima," Mrs. Sampson said, "I want you to give something to Sammy for me."

"You can give it to him yourself," Sima said. "When he comes on Sunday. That's tomorrow. Tomorrow is Sunday."

"No, Sima," she said. "I want you to give it to him."

"I'll be here. I'll take you down to see him in the lobby."

"Maybe I'll be in X-ray when he comes," Mrs. Sampson said, her head down. "You're working on Sunday, aren't you?"

"Yes."

"Well, see, there you go." She wouldn't look at Sima. "You can do it for me, then."

Mrs. Sampson lifted her pillow-hair head from the pillow. She hauled her skinny body forward, toward Sima.

"Get me my purse in the nightstand," she said.

Sima reached over and opened the cabinet. She pulled out Mrs. Sampson's big black purse. From it, Mrs. Sampson pulled out a handkerchief, a hairnet, a lipstick, a mirror, a comb, and then a little silk bag with a purple flower on the outside. She unzipped the bag and emptied it onto the white sheet between her knees. Beads dropped out, round and shiny, yellow and red and gold and green.

"My special beads," she said. "Marbles I gave to him one Christmas. He asked me to keep them for him so they wouldn't get lost."

One bead rolled away from the others. Yellow like the fiery orphan of a solid golden sun spooled against the inside pink of Mrs. Sampson's fingers. She placed the yellow bead in Sima's hand.

"I want you to give these to Sammy, in this bag."

The yellow bead was already warm. "What's he going to do with them?" Sima said.

"The beads will remind him of his grandma," she said. "I always bring these beads when we go to the natural history museum," she said. "When he gets tired of looking at the dinosaurs, we go to the cafeteria. I have a cup of tea and Sammy sits on the floor by my feet and plays with the beads, the marbles. I think he likes them more than he likes the dinosaurs."

She collected each marble off the sheet in front of her, returned each one to the little silky bag. She motioned for Sima to drop the yellow one into the bag along with the rest, and then she zipped the bag and pushed it into Sima's hand.

"Promise me, now," she squeezed Sima's hand around the bag. "Sima?"

Sima closed her fingers around the soft bag. "OK," she said. "But you can do it yourself in the morning."

Mrs. Sampson didn't say anything. She held her purse up in the air and waved it to say that Sima should put it back in the nightstand. Then she lay back on the pillow and closed her eyes.

"Mrs. Sampson?"

She kept her eyes closed and didn't say a word.

SUNDAY MORNING, THE ELEVATOR TO A71 was empty. It was Miss Lawrence's day off. Only God of the Tunnel knew how that elevator worked when it was on autopilot. Sunday, the day of rest for Catholics and Protestants, but not for Jews. Or for interns or orderlies, for that matter, Christian or otherwise. Doctors, orderlies, patients all had their schedules to follow. None of them had a day of rest.

Sima passed by the Male Room on the ward. There were three empty beds. She never saw half-empty rooms in January, when it was three days' wait in the ER to get onto a gurney, never mind into a bed, all the street people coming in from the cold. But it was June now, summer, and street people had cooler, more inviting places to lay their heads than the plastic-covered mattresses at the County.

There was only one empty bed in the Female Room. There weren't any sheets on it, just the gray mattress, a tear in the plastic near the foot end.

Sima saw Mindy leaning over a chart at the Nurses' Station.

"Hey," Sima said. "Where's Mrs. Sampson? Did someone take her to X-ray or something?"

"Or something," Mindy said. "That damn oncology fellow."

"Dr. Shum? What about him? I heard you talking to him yesterday."

Mindy lifted her head from the chart. Her post-call hairdo looked as if someone had just shot her through with an electric current. She stared straight ahead at the white wall in front of her and took a big breath. "He killed her," she said. "The jerk killed her." Her head down again, her clawed hand scribbling twisted letters on the page. She stabbed the page with the point of her pen, made a huge period in the middle of a sentence.

"What do you mean?" Sima said. "Where is she?" She could feel the bag of beads in her pocket.

"She died," Mindy said. Her shoulders sagged over the chart. "Last night. She gave up and she died."

Sima moved her leg, and the beads clicked against each other in her pocket. She could feel her heart hammering in her ears. "She gave me her beads, to give to Sammy."

Mindy kicked the Nurses' Station. "He had no right to say that to her."

"But it was the truth, wasn't it?" Sima said.

"People don't always want or need to hear the truth."

"She gave me her beads to give to Sammy," Sima said. "To give to him today."

"She knew she was going to die," Mindy said. "Patients know. They give up hope and they know. I hate when they tell me they're going to die. They always do."

"She didn't tell you that, did she?"

"She gave you her beads," Mindy said. "She told *you*."

Sima didn't want to hear that. She opened the bag and pulled out the yellow bead.

Mindy opened her hand. She poked at the yellow bead, rolled it around on her palm. "I'm not sure I can take all this truth-telling," she said.

Sima pulled out another bead, a blue one.

"You don't have to do it the way Shum does it, or anyone else for that matter," Sima said. She placed the blue bead in Mindy's palm.

"Yellow and blue make green."

"There are green ones in the bag too. Green is a secondary color."

MINDY AND SIMA WERE ALONE together in the elevator, going down. The door opened into the lobby. Not like the lobby of some fancy East Side hospital in Manhattan, marble floors and alabaster columns and valet parking. The County lobby was a few banged up chairs chained together up against the back wall. Scruffy people standing every which way—women, mostly black, holding onto little kids' hands. Waiting for visiting hours to start. There were hardly ever any men.

And there was Mrs. Sampson's good daughter, Mrs. Wilson, and Sammy. Waiting. Like the rest. On a Sunday morning. Come to visit their sick relatives. Waiting for the County cops to give them each a bright orange plastic visitor's pass that let them take the elevator and walk the hallways to wherever they had to go.

Mrs. Wilson wore sunglasses and a sleeveless blouse with small flowers on it. The blouse was tucked carefully into a maroon skirt. She held her purse in one hand, and Sammy's hand in the other. Sammy was wearing the blue shorts he had told Sima were his favorites, the ones he only wore on Sundays when he went to the natural history museum with his grandmother. Because of Mrs. Sampson's pain, they hadn't been able to go to the museum in many months now.

"Sima!" Sammy yelled. He let go of Mrs. Wilson's hand, ran to Sima's side, and took her hand. Mrs. Sampson had told him not to talk to strangers but that it was OK to hold Sima's hand.

Sima had the bag of beads in her pocket. Silky soft on the outside, and the hard, round beads clicking against each other on the inside.

Sammy was scuffing the toes of his sneakers on the linoleum floor. He looked up from the floor with his big eyes.

"Now, Sammy," Mrs. Wilson called, her voice low and serious. "Don't you be bothering Sima. I'm sure she's got a lot to do today."

"That's OK, Mrs. Wilson," Sima said. "I've got some special time for Sammy today."

Mrs. Wilson removed her sunglasses, and Sima could see that her eyes were swollen. Mindy had called her in the middle of the night when Mrs. Sampson stopped breathing. Mindy told her there was no need to rush to the hospital, and since there was no one to watch him, she could bring Sammy with her in the morning.

Mindy tipped her post-call 'do Sammy's way. "Sammy, your aunt and I have to talk," she said. She turned to Mrs. Wilson. "Is it OK if Sima gets him a donut?" she asked, her voice quiet and serious.

Mrs. Wilson nodded. She sat down on one of the chairs chained against the wall. Mindy sat down in the seat next to her and put her arm around Mrs. Wilson's shoulders.

Sima guided Sammy around so that his back was to them.

"What do you say we go get a donut?" Sima asked him, and he nodded his head yes. She led him out the side door toward the Greek truck, where, besides Danish and bagels and coffee, they sold donuts, sometimes still warm this early in the morning. There was a patch of grass there, where Sima would take Sammy to sit and eat in the sun. And then she would give him the silky bag, and they would play with the shiny beads, yellow and blue and gold and green.

Acknowledgments

So many have stood with me as teachers, friends, and loving support on the long journey from inspiration to publication. My deepest thanks to:

Dennis Johnson and Valerie Merians, co-publishers of Melville House, who chose *The Care of Strangers* as winner of the Miami Book Fair/de Groot Foundation Prize, announced with an extraordinary phone call from Clydette de Groot, and launched by the wonderful Melville House staff including Tim McCall, Selihah White, Marina Drukman, Amelia Stymacks, and Simon Reichley. Special thanks to Dennis, who called early in the COVID crisis, bunkered for two weeks in his Brooklyn garden apartment, to share his appreciation and support, and his pick for the re-envisioned title.

Alyea Canada, my remarkable editor who advocated for a title that would "identify the multiple layers of the narrative" and challenged me with big picture questions, pushing the "winning manuscript" to a deeper, more cohesive place. It was wonderful to appreciate the story through her eyes.

Tom Spanbauer, who first called me a writer when we both lived in 500 square foot walk-ups in NYC and changed my life, and the first generation of his Dangerous Writers—Joanna Rose, Carolyn Altman, Suzy Vitello, Stevan Allred, Diane Ponte, Cori-Ann Woodard, Chuck Palahniuk, among others, who listened to the very first draft ten pages a week.

Shelley Washburn, director, MFA, Pacific University, who was endlessly there, and her loving flock of faculty—Mary Helen Stefaniak, who saw the whole book in conflicts I barely recognized first semester; Claire Davis who suggested third person to tone down my borderline unreliable narrator; Bonnie Jo Campbell, thesis advisor and cycling buddy, who said I might have a novella and handed me off after graduation to her editor pal, Heidi Bell.

Natalie Serber, in her intimate Fiction Loft, who suggested the chapter title "Death Note," which became the source of the rising crisis in Sima's story.

Erin Celello, The 5th Semester mentor, who prodded me to build that crisis for Sima's change.

Deborah Reed, prolific MFA friend, who said, "You are so close. Rearrange, elevate, focus, triangulate. Then you're home free!"

Heather Sappenfield, trusted MFA friend, who admired early descriptions and scenes when there was yet no pay-off for the reader, and impelled me several years later to enter a novella contest when the manuscript was 6500 words too long.

Sue Staats, my dearest MFA friend and unending supporter, who marveled how after the lessons finally learned to release a winning manuscript that there was still more work to be done.

Tom Durkin, my loving partner and cycling companion on all roads flat or steep, short or long, for support on this project for the longest time, and my family, artists and writers among them. And my father, the first writer in my life, who cautioned, "No money in poetry," and so I finished medical school and then went on to write.

About the Author

Ellen Michaelson is a physician in Portland, Oregon and has an MFA from Pacific University. She is an assistant professor of Medicine at OHSU and vice president of the board of the Northwest Narrative Medicine Collaborative. She was an NEH Fellow in Medical Humanities and attended Breadloaf Writers Conference. Her work has appeared in *Creative Nonfiction*, *Portland Monthly*, *Literature in Medicine*, and *Women in Solitude* (SUNY Press). This is her first book.